Sumeer
Brar

October 29, 2007

The Flaming Sword

by

Sumeer Brar

authorHOUSE®

AuthorHouse™
1663 Liberty Drive, Suite 200
Bloomington, IN 47403
www.authorhouse.com
Phone: 1-800-839-8640

First published by AuthorHouse 9/26/2007

ISBN: 978-1-4343-2275-3 (sc)
ISBN: 978-1-4343-2276-0 (hc)

Printed in the United States of America
Bloomington, Indiana

This book is printed on acid-free paper.

For My Loving Parents

Author's Note

You may not know of the fabulous creatures, the Smaks, who live in a land ringed by mountains. No one knows that they are there. The Smaks themselves don't know how they got there. Perhaps the reason for this is that they have been there for as long as they can remember. A Smak looks like a boulder with arms, legs, and a head. Now the Smaks never have had any trouble from the outside. They live in communities just like ours. The Smaks began mining for gold almost as soon as they got there. One day the Smaks found that they had mined all the way to the other side of the mountain. Before I jump ahead and tell you what happens I shall have to tell you the sad fact that as our ancient ancestors had believed in them, we dismissed them along with tales of dwarves, dragons, and elves. You can hardly blame us as we came to this earth much after their time. The Klaks, that the Smaks found outside their mountains, were the main enemy of the Smaks. The Klaks look a lot like a tree, with green hair, rough brown skin, a beak so powerful, it could grind through solid rock, and also a long slender body, much like that of a tree trunk. The Klaks loved to fight the Smaks and since the Smaks were not a warring people, they did not know what to do.

Chapter 1

" The Klaks had been forgotten for a long time now" thought Suba sadly as he rolled up another scroll. He had always longed to be a hero like the ones in the stories that he read. When he was younger he dreamed Klaks would come invading and only he would be able to drive them out. Suba and Zimmo, his best friend, had always played the glorious and heroic Smaks, while Cush, Brog, and Fallou their other friends, played as the evil Klaks. Every single time the heroic Smaks won. Suba and Zimmo were still friends with Fallou and Brog though Cush had changed everything. No one had seen him for three days straight and one day Suba was walking alone through the mountains when he came across a strange looking boulder. He was going to turn it over to see if their were any strange markings on it, but when he turned it over he let out a scream and tore back down the mountain so hastily that he got many cuts and bruises. It was a whole day before he recovered enough to tell the leader of his clan that he had found Cush covered with scrapes and cuts lying dead on the mountain. It looked as if he had fallen a great height before coming to rest on that ledge. Their were also pieces of debris lying beside him. Even the leader who was known for courage and bravery looked quite shaken. Suba and Zimmo were out hunting with Lare and Kum and they brought back a lot of food since Kum and Suba were great hunters. That night when Suba got home he felt very tired after the long day's work. He dropped into the deepest sleep he'd had in a zland. [a year] When he woke up he was in the square. "That's strange," thought Suba. He did not know how he had got there. Then to his surprise, he saw his father who had died just recently, coming towards him. For a moment he forgot all his troubles and worries. He was just plain happy to see his father. But then he remembered that it must just be a dream though it went against his heart to think so. His father, Zika, beckoned for him to come closer. As he obeyed, a warm feeling came over him. But, Zika turned and said, "we must hurry you do not have much time for you to understand what you must do". In the background there was an unearthly scream. Suba then went with Zika. Zika led him up Drams Hill, the biggest hill in the clan. When they got to the top they found themselves looking down on Gucks Valley. There, in the darkness that swirled around him, Suba saw the Klaks, fighting and eating the Smaks. Zika turned and recited:

Hour by hour,
While minutes tick by,
Sun is long moon is short,

Under the bright sun,
Mourning you will be,
Melancholy too,
Eno will find the way,
Run, run if you may,
Where I shall be I shall not say.

Suba was quite scared throughout all of this and asked Zika what it meant. But Zika smiled, shook his head, and then froze in fear. Suba turned around to look, and there, only a few feet away stood a gigantic, ugly, leering Klak. In his right hand, Suba found one of the flaming swords that had been used to drive out the Klaks the first time. In his left hand he held the nightmare spear which had also been used. It was then Zika said you know what you must do. Suba could not believe it, it could not be! But even as he thought it, he knew that it must be so. He turned to face the Klak, raised his spear high and held the sword at ready. As the Klak rushed him, he knew he could take him. It was as if his senses had been heightened. The Klak spun his javelin around and stabbed at Suba's right. Suba slashed down with the sword, and as he made contact deflecting the javelin, the Klak's javelin caught fire. The Klak screamed and dropped the weapon. Then Suba raised his spear. The Klak laughed, a chilling sound, and raised his shield fearlessly. Suba stabbed forward striking true against the Klak's shield. Suba's spear bounced back, but where the Klak's shield had been a moment ago, there was nothing. The Klak looking extremely surprised and fled. Suba then found a bow in his hand with a quiver full of arrows strapped to his back. He strung and nocked an arrow. He took careful aim with an arrow that was freezing and burning at the same time. The arrow went straight through the Klak killing him instantly, while the arrow that Suba had shot had come back to him. When Suba turned to look for his father, he found no one there. He yelled into the night "where are these?" On a breath of the wind he heard a voice saying "go on a journey and you will know." But then as the darkness swirled around him, he saw in quick succession, a mountain, a forest, and a cloud. He saw no more after that and woke to the sunshine and peace of his own bed.

Chapter 2

Suba went to take his daily shower, while debating whether or not to tell Zimmo about his dream. He thought that it could only have been a dream, but then he thought that it might be reality. In the end he decided to tell Zimmo. When he went to the clock tower where he said he would meet Zimmo, Brog, and Fallou, Zimmo was already there.

"Zimmo, Zimmo you'll never believe what happened!"

"What?" cried Zimmo.

As Suba started telling Zimmo about his dream, he could see Zimmo's eyes grow wider than plates. He asked, "do you think we should tell the other's?"

"Yeah they'll probably want to know."

Then their friends appeared right on time. Together Suba and Zimmo alternately told about it. Fallou looked amazed, but Brog only looked thoughtful.

"Brog? I think you know something that you aren't telling."

"My dad told me about this old gigantic volcano and according to legend, there was an amazing treasure hidden there." At this, Suba grew suddenly excited and said, "the flaming sword could be hidden there!" When he asked how far away was it, Brog said 5 days of easy traveling.

"Well then what are we waiting for" said Suba. Suba noticed that Fallou did not look excited. He asked her about it.

Fallou said, "I'll come but I'm not sure that we should be doing this". Just when they were ready to go, Fallou came up to Suba and said "we're not going." Suba looked at her in surprise.

"It's not that I don't want to go it's only I realized something that you didn't. Going down your father's rhyme said H W SUMMER W. Therefore I think that we should leave during the summer on a special date like midsummer." Suba had to agree that this was reasonable logic.

Then Zimmo came and said, "the rhyme also says that Eno will find the way. Even though we don't know anyone named Eno, I think we should wait." Suba then asked Fallou if she had gotten any other bright ideas.

"Actually I have. We should try to leave right at midsummer since we have everything already packed. Zimmo added "we should still leave at night since we do not want to be seen as the elders would just laugh at them and say that it was just a dream.

When midsummer night finally rolled around and they all met, Zimmo looked excited.

Suba said "I know it's exciting but try to calm down." Zimmo brought out five assorted weapons from behind his back. He had a mace, a sword, a bow and a quiver full of arrows, a spear, and an axe. He also had shields for each weapon. Suba wanted the sword, Zimmo wanted the spear, Brog wanted the axe, and Fallou wanted the bow and the arrows. While Zimmo was giving out the weapons and the shields

Suba asked "why did you bring an extra weapon and shield?"

Zimmo just shrugged and said "remember Eno?"

Suba smiled sheepishly and said "I ought to start thinking like you are." Right when they were ready to move Brog came hurrying back from his post as lookout and whispered " I've seen two lanterns in the distance that are coming closer every minute. We have to move now!" When the wagon was rolling, Suba looked back at the city and thought about the only home he had ever known and sighed.

Chapter 3

*E*no didn't know why he had awoken at the crack of dawn. He was up before everyone else. He snuck outside to the field of corn as he often did. In the distance over the fire mountain the sun's first rays were streaking down over the mountain's twin peaks, Vamor and Pilisk, illuminating a wagon and making it look golden. In a flash Eno's dream came back to him. A golden wagon that he had to get on. The Smaks inside needed him. He did not know the reason why. He only knew that the future of Smakkind rested within that wagon.

* * *

Suba got out of the wagon as soon as he woke up without telling the others. When he got outside he saw a figure running toward him faster than he had ever seen anyone go. Though the figure was not even the size of his pinkie finger yet, it was growing at an alarming rate. Suba ran back inside the wagon shouting "Everyone wake up, wake up! We've been spotted!"

While Zimmo and Brog took a while to get up, Fallou jumped up and help to start moving away from the figure that was now the size of a regular Smak and a mere hundred yards away. By now Brog and Zimmo were wide awake and asking what was going on. Suba only yelled "help us go faster we've been spotted!" Brog leaped up to help while Zimmo went to the window to see the figure.

"I can see him clearly he's only twenty yards away!"

"What! Go faster, faster!" Fallou said "we might be able to lose him." Zimmo shouted back that the Smak was only ten yards away and closing. All of a sudden, Brog had a great idea.

"Fallou! Use the arrows that Zimmo gave you!" Fallou quickly got them out. As she was taking aim, the figure let out a yell. "I am a friend." Fallou took careful aim and drew her bowstring. As the figure stumbled on, Suba had a terrible thought. He dived at Fallou and knocked the bow out of her hands just as she fired. It threw her aim of a little bit and instead of hitting the Smak in the heart as she had intended it to, it went just wide and hit him in the shoulder. As the figure stumbled and fell close to the wagon, Suba leaped down of the moving wagon and rolled as he hit the ground. The others stopped the wagon immediately. Suba leveled his sword at the Smak and walked towards the heap on the ground. As Eno had barely enough energy to stand he only managed to whisper 'Eno' before he fainted. Only Suba had heard this and his sword clattered to the ground in surprise.

"This is who will find the way." He turned around and held up his hands saying that they did not need to attack, but heal him. As the others learned that this was Eno, they all stood silently. But then, Zimmo whispered "our group is complete."

Chapter 4

After Eno was healed from his exhaustion and arrow wound which didn't take long, he looked up to find Suba looking at him.

"Who are you?" asked Eno. Suba stared and stated plainly, "I'm Suba." Eno then asked what he was doing and where he was going. Suba said to the volcano. Eno looked at him as if he was crazy. Suba jumped when a voice at his shoulder said "the fire mountain." He turned around and saw Zimmo standing behind him. "That was what the people from the village we just passed called the volcano. Suba laughed, something that he had not done in quite a while, and said, "what would I do without you." As soon as Zimmo had said the fire mountain, Eno's eyes had brightened. Suba asked him, "do you know about the fire mountain?" Eno nodded. "whenever a young Smak in our village is in their first year of manhood they journey to the fire mountain and stay there for a week, praying. It is known

13

that you are a strong man if you come back after a week of praying and fighting monsters. My village is also kept fit by these journeys. It's also my time to go so I won't be missed." The last thing that he said was that there path would be marked by many dangers and obstacles. After saying this Eno dropped into a deep sleep. As the day went by and their wagon rumbled on, Suba got very bored and in the warm sun, he slowly fell asleep. Then as Suba later reflected he must have had a dream because he heard a voice commanding him to rise. He moaned not wanting to get up yet but the voice returned with even more intensity. He finally rose. As he groggily got to his feet, he realized that night had fallen. He also thought he heard quiet, almost muffled footsteps. He tapped Fallou's back and told her to wake the others as soon as she got up. When everyone was up he asked Zimmo, who had been driving the wagon, where they were. Zimmo hesitantly answered and when he did, he muttered something so quietly that no one heard him. When Suba asked again, Zimmo said that they were at the edge of the Ragger. A collective gasp went through the small group and Brog whispered "*the* Ragger? The one where all the Zakos [bandits] hide? The one that's so dangerous no one has ever even tried to go through and lived except the Blackbow?" Zimmo simply nodded. "Why?" shouted Fallou before Suba could tell her not to yell. Zimmo said that they had arrived at the edge of the rocky and dangerous mountain region just as darkness had fallen. He knew that they would not have been able to go through the region at nighttime, so he decided to camp at the edge. Suba started frantically gesturing for everyone to be quiet and grab their weapon. As soon as everyone had everything that they needed, he told them about the footsteps he'd heard and the voice in his dream. Eno laughed nervously and told Suba that he sure could make good jokes. "If I am joking then, pointing towards the end of the wagon with his sword which he had just unsheathed, who are they?" said Suba Where Suba had pointed, there were zakos pouring into the wagon.

Chapter 5

*Z*immo grabbed his spear from a nearby shelf and jumped up beside Suba. Brog grabbed his axe's hilt from where it lay and quickly hefted it. Fallou, whose arrows would be no use at the close range, grabbed a medium –sized log from the fire which had just gone out. But it was Eno who struck the first blow. He spun his mace's chain and wrapped it around the legs of one of the zakos. The spiked ball at the end of the chain dug into the zakos' leg and brought him crashing and screaming to the ground, tripping a few other zakos. Then Suba launched himself into the battle. When Suba had gone, Zimmo and Brog looked at each other and Zimmo said "good luck" and Brog replied "you too" and charged. Fallou hung at the edge, not really wanting to join in. Once, when Zimmo passed Suba, he noticed that Suba's eyes were blood red and that he was crushing anybody who stood in his path. This was quite unlike the Suba that Zimmo knew and Zimmo wondered what had happened to his lifelong friend. The battle had ended quite quickly since the zakos' numbers were not many and Suba and Eno had some surprising talent. Zimmo asked Suba to come to one side of the wagon. Zimmo quietly whispered to Suba about what he had seen in the battle. Suba said "I don't remember much of it." Brog had heard Zimmo's question and he said "I read about that in an ancient book. It is called the bloodlust and only great heroes or heroes to be get it. In battle it can help you a whole lot. For instance, your senses are multiplied by about five and your speed is doubled and last of all you get three times stronger. But it also comes at a price. It is hard to distinguish who is friend or foe and the person who has it will crush anyone in their path including friends." Zimmo sat in stunned silence. Suba just wondered. To any body else it would look as if Suba was just normal. But inside he was wondering that if he was chosen that meant he had a mission to fill. That night Suba could not stop thinking about the bloodlust. He tossed and turned so much that Brog, who was sleeping next to him, got quite mad and threw a pillow at him. When Suba finally managed to fall asleep, his dreams were troubled. When Suba got up the next morning he saw Brog driving the wagon instead of Zimmo. Brog had told Zimmo that he had better drive considering last nights events. Suba tried to get back to sleep but it was no use. He got up and looked around. Only Brog was up. Suba walked over to Brog and put a hand on his shoulder which made Brog jump. Brog turned around and said "never do that again."

"How much longer do you think it will take to reach the fire mountain?"

"We should arrive later today providing that the weather's good and no one else takes it into their head to attack us. I don't think that anyone will after last night." Brog cast a sideways glance at Suba. When Suba looked outside the wagon, all he could see was what looked like an endless plain stretching out before them and going to meet the sky. In the sky he thought he saw something huge flying around. He turned around to wake up Fallou and Zimmo, thinking that maybe Fallou's arrows could reach it. When he turned around, he found them right behind him. Zimmo said "as always, one step ahead of you" and smiled in a sly way. Suba got mad at Zimmo at dived at him playfully. Behind them Fallou took careful aim, and fired. A moment later she screamed "I think we have a problem!"

Chapter 6

Suba and Zimmo stopped rolling around on the floor. Brog and Eno woke up with a start and said "what's the shouting for?" Fallou pointed at the sky. And there, way up high but diving was a gigantic *thing* that was headed straight for them! Suba asked Fallou about her arrow.

"The thing picked it right up out of the air and broke it in half!"

"Let's get out of here and start running" said Zimmo. Brog, Zimmo, Eno, and Fallou jumped down right away, but Suba stayed. He was very curious about the thing even though he knew it would most likely be dangerous. Zimmo hung back for a minute yelling for Suba to get moving. But Suba would not be swayed. Finally Zimmo gave up on him because he was so scared. By this time the thing was a lot closer, close enough to see what it looked like. While Suba stared up at it, it opened its mouth and two things came out. One was the biggest and loudest roar that Suba had ever heard. It almost broke his eardrums. The other thing that came out perplexed Suba much more. Burning hot flames erupted from the creature's mouth. It shocked Suba so much that he fell backwards into a corner of the wagon. The dragon (for Suba was sure that was what the thing was) swerved around so that it now ran parallel to the ground and was coming at the wagon from a different direction altogether. Suba drew his sword as the dragon approached. By now he could see that the dragon had glittering scales colored a beautiful emerald green. Suba jumped down from the wagon with his sword held in front of him thinking that maybe the dragon would go for the wagon since it was bigger. The dragon did not decide to go after the wagon but turned and faced Suba. The dragon came closer till it was right above him. Suba held his sword up high and faced the dragon. One of the dragon's hind legs reached down and grabbed Suba effortlessly. Since Suba's arms were free and he still had his sword he began hacking anywhere he could reach on the dragon's leg. Soon he realized that the dragon's scales stopped him from doing any real hurt to the dragon. Up close, Suba realized that the dragon was simply colossal. It was about the size of a small hill. Suba had only heard of dragons in legend but he had never heard of them in fact and he did not know anyone that believed in dragons. Suba didn't know what to expect, if the dragon could talk, or even if it was intelligent. The dragon's wings were about 15 feet long and 5 feet wide and had spikes running along the edges. With every flap wind buffeted Suba. The dragon's emerald scales glittered so brightly it seemed as if they were made of light. It had two long hind legs, and two shorter fore legs. Each of its legs ended in sharpened talons. The dragon's tail was very long and ended in spikes. There were also spikes running down the dragon's neck that started at the back of its neck and went all the way down to its tail. There was roughly two and a half feet between each spike. Suba didn't know what he was supposed to do so he said "who are you?" He knew that he couldn't expect to hear anything in return but he decided to say something anyways. Surprisingly, he did get an answer though he did not hear anything. A voice echoed around in his head.

"I am Sobask" said the voice in his head. Shocked, scared, and excited at the same time, Suba thought "what are you?" *"You have not guessed as much? I expected much more. I am a dragon."* "I knew that" disputed Suba hotly. Then he calmed down remembering who he was talking to. "Are you going to eat me or hurt me in any way?" *"What,"* said Sobask and made a weird sort of noise, which after a minute Suba realized was laughter. The dragon finally said,

"Eat you? Of course not. You are much too important for that. Besides, we get all the strength we need from flying."

"Where are you taking me?" Suba asked. *"Patience is a virtue"* replied Sobask. Even as darkness began to descend, Sobask flew on.

Chapter 7

Zimmo, Brog, Eno, and Fallou had watched helplessly as Suba had been taken by the thing, whatever it was. Brog had wanted to rush right after the thing and take it apart, limb by limb and Zimmo and Fallou had to hold him back. While Zimmo struggled to stop Brog from going after the beast, Fallou tried to reason with him.

"You can not go out there Brog. You saw how easily it dealt with Suba." At long last Brog stopped struggling.

"You are right" said Brog. But Zimmo said that they had to follow the beast but they should do it in stealth rather than make a mad dash straight after it. Everyone had to agree that it was a good plan, and as no one could think of any better plan, they set off into the brush, keeping there heads down. Unknown to them, a small party of Goven, who had been tracking them, halted. Goven were strong and muscular even if they were slow and clumsy. They stood at least a head taller than the Smaks.

Their sickly green skin was very wrinkly. The Goven had not been seen since the Hero Smaks of old had driven them deep within the mountains and sealed them in. They were here on the orders of their master who had told them to follow the party of Smaks and give back reports. Their general, General Blask was a tough and vicious looking Goven. He had become General by killing the earlier general. There had been many attempts to assassinate him, each one coming to nothing. Blask had horns that stuck straight up from his head and were tipped with poison. One stab from them and you were done for. He kicked a Goven near and shouted "up you mangy excuses for Goven, March!" The group, terrified of their leader's wrath was up in the blink of an eye. It was night, but that was when the Goven were strongest. Blask yelled for the group to halt after awhile, and sent two scouts up ahead. When they did not come back, he sent his entire troop forward when they stumbled on the other Goven they found them both lying on the ground, dead. One of them had an arrow stuck in him the other had violent looking wounds all over his body. They looked like the work of an axe, a spear, or both. Blask stared into the darkness surrounding them and whispered 'whoever you are, I shall hunt you to the ends of the Earth and back if I have to, but I will have revenge for this!'

* * *

Zimmo, Brog, Eno, and Fallou had been struggling through the brush, when Zimmo said in a strangely high voice "this is a good place to rest" and promptly sat down. Fallou, Eno and Brog took the cue and sat down. Immediately Zimmo whispered, almost without moving his lips, 'Don't look now but something is following us.' Of course they all looked. One green shape flashed out of the trees and began to run. Fallou was just getting out her bow, yet she knew she wouldn't have time to use it. Before she even had unslung it from her back, something silver flashed at the side of her. The silver thing was headed straight for the green shape. As she realized that, the silver thing hit the green shape and it stumbled, and then went down. Fallou stood up to tell Zimmo before she realized that Zimmo had thrown his spear with incredible accuracy. When she turned around again she saw a flicker of movement in a bush. But this time when the shape started running, she was ready. She brought her bow up, and fired. The shape went down immediately. Brog and Zimmo had run after the first figure. Brog had his axe drawn, and when they reached the figure as it was still alive, started chopping the figure up and would have gone on forever if Zimmo hadn't stopped him. "Whoa buckoe it's dead already" Zimmo said, and pulled Brog off the shape. Meanwhile Fallou and Eno went after the other figure, Fallou had an arrow nocked on her string, but when she got there she found the figure already dead with an arrow in its back. She was disgusted and went towards the place were the other figure had fallen with Eno. When they got there they found the other figure dead and Zimmo fighting with Brog to keep him off the figure. Fallou and Eno jumped in and helped to hold Brog till he calmed down. After that Fallou asked Zimmo how he knew that they were enemies. Zimmo said "I knew of those creatures. They are called Goven and they are evil. They used to kill Smaks." Fallou shuddered when she took in what Zimmo said.

Chapter 8

Sobask had finally reached his destination. Suba was sleeping when they got there. Sobask gently shook Suba awake and pointed one talon into the darkness. Even though Suba strained his eyes, he could see nothing.

"Alas, I forget how weak your human eyes are" said Sobask. He began moving forward until Suba let out a gasp. There, in the darkness, were three shapes standing out. One was holding a bow pointed straight at them. The next was holding a javelin poised at the moment of throwing. The last one was holding a sword frozen while cleaving downwards. Suba reacted instinctively and ducked down beneath one of Sobask's spikes. Sobask laughed and said, *"there is no need to be afraid. The guardians are only alive to our enemies."* Suba was shocked. There were so many questions buzzing around in his head it felt like a river of questions had just burst into his head. He hardly knew where to start. Finally, he decided on a question which he

had wanted to ask for a while now. 'Sobask, are you able to use magic?' Sobask inclined his head. *"To some degree, yes."* This remark led to a series of questions bursting forth from Suba which had to be stopped by Sobask.

"The only thing that I will tell you is that we picked you for a reason. You have magical abilities that you have not yet discovered. The rest of your questions will soon be answered." And in the darkness that was night, Suba thought that he could make out a shape coming up in the darkness.

Chapter 9

Ganuf was not in a good mood. And when Ganuf was not in a good mood, you did not want to be anywhere close to him. Ganuf was a dark wizard. But not just any dark wizard. He was the strongest, fiercest, and most cunning wizard alive. If he got mad at you, your life would be over. At this moment he was standing at a window in the highest room of his tower. His glittering black robe and hat went well with his eyes. Pure black, like the darkest pit of evil. Some said that if you looked into them you would be hypnotized and have no control over yourself. His tower was something built of nightmares. It was black with zigzagging streaks of red going down, looking very much like a bloody finger pointing at the sky. Ganuf's minions, the Goven, were cowering down at the very bottom of the tower, each hoping their leader's rage would not be vented on them. Ganuf was not in a good mood for one simple reason, he had not got a report back from the group of Goven he had set tailing the Smaks. He made a mental note to lower General Blask, who was the leader of the group

While he was thinking these thoughts, a ripple appeared in the air in front of him. This marked a report coming back. Maybe he would not have to lower General Blask. He was a good General. The air in front of Ganuf suddenly solidified into a disk that a face could be seen through. General Blask could be seen talking to one other Goven. When he realized that Ganuf was watching him, he quickly turned around to face him. Ganuf just watched. Blask stuttered and said, "Sir two goven scouts were killed when I sent them forward. That is the only unusual happening to report sir." Ganuf grunted and turned around thinking. Blask was still there and didn't know what to do. "Sir?"

Ganuf roared in fury and spun around blasting a ball of fire out of his fingertips. . Blask screamed in pain as the fiery ball struck his face, burning him badly. Ganuf angrily closed the communication disk. This was very bad news. If even one of the party of smaks knew anything about history, they could figure out that a group of goven were following them. This only worsened Ganuf's temper. He teleported himself downstairs and summoned a goven who was nearby to follow him. The trembling individual had to follow. Ganuf took him to his room and magically closed the door and locked it. The trembling goven was nearly scared out of his wits. He had heard what his master would do to you if he was not in a good mood. So he had good reason to be afraid. Ganuf told the unfortunate goven to go to the window and look outside. The goven, whose name was

Ranum, went. There, Ganuf raised his hand and blasted Ranum with dark lightning. Ranum fell screaming out the window. Ganuf laughed then, a chilling sound it was. He was happy with his growing power.

Chapter 10

E no, Brog, Zimmo, and Fallou had started walking again right after they saw the Goven. Zimmo thought they should put as much distance as possible between them and the Goven. He knew that they were not very fast, and if they got a little bit ahead of the Goven, the Goven would not be able to catch up. So they set of and kept on going. Now the Smaks were not as fast as Sobask, but they were persistent and kept with it. So they were very close to where Suba and Sobask had landed. They came to a place where Eno found the ground looking torn up as if gouged by claws. Brog said "the creature that had taken Suba had long, sharp claws. I bet this is where they landed!" Then Fallou yelled "What are we waiting for" and charged off. Eno, Brog, and Zimmo set off after her and tried to get her to quiet down and come back but she was fast. Then Fallou came tearing back down the hill they were going up and told them to get down. They got down and Zimmo asked "What's wrong with you Fallou?"

"Get out your weapons and follow me, quietly!" They went up the hill very slowly, and when they got to the top, it seemed as if the climb had taken hours. Then Brog asked rather loudly "what's the matter Fallou?" Fallou desperately motioned for him to be quiet, brought up her bow and fired. Then they all saw why Fallou had come back. There were three gigantic figures standing there. One had a bow and was pointing it at them. The next had a javelin ready to be thrust at them. The last one had a sword that was cleaving downwards at them. Fallou's arrow headed straight for the one holding the spear and struck it in the stomach. But there was a ringing sound and Fallou's arrow bounced right off. Fallou was shocked. Eno ran forward swinging his mace and Brog took out his axe and ran after Eno. Only Zimmo did nothing. Fallou looked over at him and yelled for him to help in the fight while firing arrows off like crazy. But Zimmo shook his head. Then she realized that he was laughing. She stopped firing, turned to him and said "do you know something we don't? Because even if you don't you sure aren't smart not to fight!" she screamed. Zimmo, still laughing, nodded. Fallou got up and shook Zimmo. "What, what" she cried. Zimmo, who was still shaking with mirth, pointed at the figures which had not moved. "They're stone!" Fallou stared at him dumbstruck.

"*What!*"

"Aye" said Zimmo. Eno and Brog, who had realized that by know, trudged back looking rather sheepish. Zimmo laughed

36

and laughed then finally stopped and the little party decided to camp at that spot for the night.

Chapter 11

Suba had kept wide awake on Sobask for a long time. He was ready to go to sleep when he saw the mammoth structure standing in the dark. He quietly asked Sobask what it was.

"It is what you have been seeking. I am surprised that you could not see it before. It is what you call the fire mountain." Suba was amazed.

"This is the fire mountain? Sure doesn't like what I saw in my dream."

"That is because it is dark now you can rest till the sun comes out again. Do not worry, I will wake you." Suba immediately lay down and promptly fell asleep. The next morning Suba was rudely awakened by a roaring in his head that was so loud he could have sworn that if someone else had been nearby they would have heard it too. He got up and looked around. He saw Sobask who looked a little smug.

"I told you I would wake you." Suba just shook his head and looked at the fire mountain. It was gigantic. It went up on an angle going to the top. But when it got there it split into twin peaks which made it look very much like a pointed horseshow sitting on a mountain. It was breathtaking. He was where he had been trying to get. If only Fallou, Eno, Brog, and Zimmo were here it would be perfect. But they weren't and for some reason Suba did not want to go in without them. But just at that moment, with perfect timing, they showed up. They had their weapons out. Fallou fired an arrow but Suba jumped up and sliced it in half with his sword, once more displaying his excellent swordsmanship. Fallou yelled for him to turn around but Suba said "no, wait! He is a friend." Eno, Brog, Zimmo, and Fallou came slowly up the hill and all of a sudden began chattering like crazy. But Suba saw something and yelled for them to stop. He drew his sword pointed it at the bushes and said in a clear, strong voice "what do you want." Then about forty green shapes burst out of the bushes and headed straight for them. Zimmo moaned. "Goven and so many of them." Fallou started firing arrows of into their midst, cutting down a good many of them. By the time the Goven who were slow and clumsy got to the top of the hill, Fallou had cut there numbers down to about twenty. These were still going to be too many for their small band. Suba strode forward followed by Brog and Zimmo. Together they formed a triangle, one shield to the next, weapons bristling through the gaps in their wall of shields. Fallou was ready to fire arrows over their heads, when Sobask sent a thought to Suba. *"Let me handle these. I need some fun."*

Suba, surprised by this sent back, "fun?" "There are so many!" But still, Suba told everyone to stop. They looked at him like he was crazy, but at that moment, Sobask sent a gust of flame that instantly killed ten Goven. Then he jumped over the Smaks and landed among the Goven. Sobask's talons and jaws were a whirlwind of death. Within moments, he had killed the last Goven. Suba and the other Smaks stood in awe. After a while Suba turned and motioned to the others to follow him. He turned towards the fire mountain and was about to start towards it when there was a crack and a tall Smak appeared. Suba jumped back in shock and instinctively brought up his sword. "Who are you" he asked. The stranger said "I could ask you the same yet I am Ganuf." Suba kept his sword up as there was something he did not trust about Ganuf. In this time Brog, Zimmo, Eno, and Fallou had caught up. They too had their weapons out. In the back Suba could feel Sobask stiffen then yell at him *"run you fool, he is evil!"* Suba half-turned before he was blasted to the ground. Suba raised his head to look around and saw Zimmo laying flat on his back, unmoving. Fallou's arm was stuck out at a weird angle. Brog's axe had cut deep into his leg. Eno's mace had one point embedded deep in the ground and the spiked ball had wrapped around him, rendering him immobile. Suba slowly got to his feet and turned to face Ganuf who was smiling. Suba picked up his sword and charged Ganuf, but Ganuf raised his arm and swept it outwards. It was as if a shock wave had blasted out from Ganuf. Suba was caught and flung backwards. Suba got to his feet again, slower this time. Then without any warning he ran back straight at Ganuf. Ganuf raised his hand and Suba

41

saw that a ball of dark energy had gathered at the palm of his hand. By now Suba was getting very close to Ganuf. But Ganuf raised his hand and pointed it at Suba. The ball flew of his hand and struck Suba square in the chest. Suba was blasted of his feet and thrown backwards. Amazingly, Suba staggered to get to his feet again. Suba looked around wondering what had happened to Sobask. Then he turned and saw him hanging in midair, motionless. Then Suba turned around to look at Ganuf who was just standing there. He slowly got up and began walking towards him. Ganuf threw another ball of dark energy at him that Suba dodged, but another came. This time Suba reacted out of instinct. The arm holding his sword came down right as the ball was ready to strike him. Suba's sword struck the ball and the ball disappeared. Then something strange happened Ganuf began firing balls of the four elements: fire, water, earth, and air. Finally, Ganuf got frustrated. All of a sudden Suba could not move at all. Then Ganuf laughed and said "sorry I have to do this ... not!" He sent a web of golden light arching over Suba, Zimmo, Brog, Fallou, Eno, and Sobask. There was a flash of golden light and everything was gone.

Chapter 12

Suba woke up to find a spike sticking up in front of his face. He yelled and started crawling back as far as he could. Soon Suba's head hit a pair of feet. He craned his neck to look up and saw Zimmo smiling at him. In a flash last nights events came back to him. He jumped up and looked around for Ganuf. Zimmo smiled again and told him that Ganuf had teleported them. Suba looked around again.

"What" he said.

"We figured that out while you were knocked out" Zimmo said. Suba looked around. Sure enough the fire mountain was nowhere in sight.

"But then where are we" asked Suba.

"And where is the fire mountain, how are we going to get back to it?"

"Do not worry I can carry you and your friends back. Carrying all of them will slow me down a bit but I will still

be able to take all of you back. I am not yet strong enough
to teleport all of you." Suba finally began to relax for a while
thinking back to what had happened last night. He decided that
he would ask Sobask what to do if he had to fight a wizard ever
again. But not right now. Sobask had other things to do. Suba
thought that he had better help get ready the things they would
need for the trip. But when he got up to actually help, Fallou
said smiling "get some sleep Suba, we've already packed. You
can sleep on Sobask." Just when everyone was finally ready to
go. Suba thought that he had better ask Sobask.

"Sobask, how am I going to defeat Ganuf if he knows magic?
I mean I can't do something that he can, can I?"

*"Dear me! What am I thinking letting you go of to fight him
without even the slightest training in magic!"*

"I can use magic? " asked Suba.

*"Yes along with one other. I shall have to take you two to a
place where you can train in your magical abilities. I also know
a place where we can keep your friends till we finish. They will
be happy there."*

"Wait, you said two of us would go. Who else is coming?"

"Eno." Sobask spoke the word softly. Suba wondered
if this would mean anything or not. Suba got up to tell the
others, outwardly appearing calm, but inwardly bubbling with
excitement. First he decided he would tell just Eno, and then
tell the others all at one time. He went to Eno and asked if he
could see him for a minute. Eno raised an eyebrow but followed
Suba a little way away from the camp. Suba stared at Eno for a
while wondering how to tell him. Eno sat there and finally asked

"what?" It all poured out of Suba then as if the words were eager to get out. 'You-and I-are-magical-and-Sobask-is-going-to-take-us-to-a-place-where-we-will-train-with-magic. Eno looked at him for a minute then laughed out loud.

"What, us, magical?" He sounded like he half believed Suba.

"Sure." Suba just stared levelly at him for a time then went back to Sobask. Eno came rushing after him.

"You're not serious, are you? Because if you are…" he trailed of into silence. They had reached camp. Sobask said *"I have already told the others. I took them to the place I told you about using a bit of my magic. Is Eno ready?"*

"Yeah I guess so" said Suba.

"Come on Eno." As he said that, a tiny jolt went through him. He, Suba was going to learn magic! Beside him, Suba noticed that Eno's eyes were wide with excitement. They both hopped on Sobask, with Eno in the front and Suba right behind him.

"How long do you think it is going to take us to get there Sobask?"

"No time at all. I shall just use some magic to get us there."

"Um, Sobask. Whose going to be our teacher, are you?"

"Me! Why of course not! You shall meet your teacher when you arrive there. Now be prepared for me to use some magic. It might be a bit disconcerting for you two since you have never used or felt magic before. Since there are only two of you, I should be strong enough to teleport all of us." Suba gave Eno

Sobask's warning but even he was not prepared for what he felt after that. There was a horrible feeling that he was being squeezed. In the beginning it wasn't so bad. But after a while of continual squeezing he began to feel he would be crushed soon. Suba couldn't see a thing. He tried to turn his head and see what was happening to Eno but he couldn't. When the crushing feeling was starting to hurt *really* bad Suba was almost certain that Sobask had made a mistake. Just when it got to the point that Suba thought he would never come out of it, it stopped. Immediately after that there was the immensely pleasurable feeling of not being squeezed. Suba just wanted to lay on that grass for a while and go to sleep. But he forced himself to get up and look around. What he saw shocked him. He had arrived at the academy!

Chapter 13

Suba stared in shock. The academy, for that's what the sign said it was, was huge. It was also an amazing structure of quite daring architecture. First there was a walk leading up to it. In the middle of the walk there was a grand fountain that had a sculpture made of ice on top of it. Behind that the Academy of Magic loomed. On either side of the tall oaken doors jets of water shot around, bouncing in arcs. The Academy itself looked something like a castle. It had many turrets and towers. It even had its own moat and drawbridge. After Suba got over his initial shock he looked over at Eno who was staring openmouthed at the Academy. Suba turned around and blinked hard, but when looked, the Academy was still there. He closed his eyes and rubbed them and opened them again. The Academy was still there. Suba looked over at Eno again and this time saw Eno looking back. Suba gave Eno a grin that Eno returned.

"Well, shall we go in?" Suba turned to ask Sobask but saw that he was not there.

"Look Eno, Sobask's gone." Eno was just about to turn when Suba caught hold of his sleeve.

"There's someone coming out to meet us." The Smak, if that's what he was very tall. He had a blue wizard's hat and cape and was carrying a worn weather beaten staff that had a curious blue ball on top of it. As he came nearer and nearer, Suba and Eno began walking towards him. When they finally met him, he stood silently staring at them before asking "are you the two Sobask was talking about?" Suba said that yes indeed they were. The Smak chuckled and said "well come in, come in. Even we show hospitality!" Suba and Eno started walking towards the academy following the other Smak. After a while of silent walking, Eno decided to break the silence.

"Sir, we don't know you're name."? The Smak chuckled.

"There's no need to "sir" me." My name is Raguf and you may call me that." By now Suba, Eno, and Raguf had reached the front door. Raguf put his hand on the door and in a moment, it opened by no means that Suba or Eno could see. But what they saw after that took their breath away. The ceiling was so high you could just barely see it. The room that they were facing was circular, and had about a three hundred foot circumference. But in that room, there were about two hundred doors branching out of it. That wasn't all though. Smaks were speeding in and out of doorways without moving a muscle! Before Suba or Eno could ask about this Raguf turned to them smiling and said "I take it that you are wondering about a great many things. But now is not the time to ask them. I am to take you to our head wizard. All your questions will be answered there." Then Raguf held them both tightly and said "to Sangun." Immediately, Suba and Eno felt themselves speeding forward like the other wizard Smaks. There were many twists and turns but it did not make Suba feel the slightest bit dizzy. In fact, it made him feel exhilarated. He looked over at Eno to see the same feelings mirrored on his face. Soon their ride came to a stop. Neither Suba nor Eno was expecting it so they both tumbled out onto the floor of a very spacious room. Before they could lift their heads a voice said "ah, so you are here."

Chapter 14

Suba and Eno looked up to see a very old Smak smiling at them. He was wearing wizard's clothes and carrying a staff that had a pure white ball on top of it. Suba looked around to see Raguf standing smiling. Once again, before Suba or Eno could say anything Sangun, if he was the head wizard, spoke.

"I know we are rushing you into many things but bear with me. You see the ball on top of my staff? How it is white? Well, that tells you my strength is wind. There is earth, fire, ice, wind, water, darkness, and light. Don't say anything yet. It is time for you two to learn your powers." Sangun unlocked a chest in the back of the room that Suba and Eno had not seen before. Sangun took out a staff of all the powers he had mentioned. Then he told Eno to hold all of the staff's one at a time. Eno took them but nothing happened at any of them. The same thing happened with Suba. Raguf was quite disappointed. He said "maybe they do not have magical powers after all Sangun. Sobask could have made a mistake." But Sangun was looking thoughtful and rather hopeful thought Suba.

"There is one staff left Raguf" said Sangun. Raguf was awed. Sangun reached deep into the chest and brought out a staff that had a rainbow colored ball on top of it. Then he said "hold this Suba, but treat it gently for it is the most powerful staff of all." Suba reached for it and as soon as his fist closed around it, he felt a wild, happy power rushing through him. A blaze of light had erupted from the staff also. When the light subsided, Suba looked around. Raguf and Sangun were looking astonished and Eno was just looking bewildered. Sangun quickly reached into the chest and brought another rainbow staff out for Eno to try. The same thing that had happened with Suba happened to Eno. Sangun and Raguf were really looking amazed now. Suba asked "um, what kind of staff is that. You never told us anything about a rainbow colored ball on top of one."

"That is the staff of everything. You two command all the powers! No one has done that since Shaduf the greatest wizard of all time was alive!" Suba said "that's all very great sir but I have a feeling Ganuf is trying to get the flaming sword also. That can be the only reason he wanted us out of the way. So, about how long does magic training take?"

"Oh, about two to three years" said Raguf. Suba stared at him in dismayed shock. "But we don't have that kind of time! Ganuf will probably get the sword in a month or two at the most!"

"Relax my friend" said Sangun.

"I have a thing that just might do the trick." Sangun reached into a drawer on his desk and brought out two amulets. There was a sharp intake of breath from Raguf.

"You are going to use those? They might be one of the most powerful things you have Sangun!"

"Ah but there mission is also very important Raguf." Eno looked from Raguf to Sangun.

"Could someone please fill me in here? I don't understand. What's so special about those amulets?" Raguf looked shocked but Suba said "yes, tell us." Raguf said quite breathlessly "it teaches you everything that there is to learn of magic in one second! But it can only be used once though and it only works while you are wearing it. But it doesn't really teach you magic spells. It just makes you learn how to use magic. That and the fact that it is so rare make it very valuable indeed." Sangun reached into his desk.

"Not to worry Raguf." And he brought out three other amulets. Raguf stood in shocked amazement with his mouth hanging open. Sangun handed two of the amulets to Suba who gave one to Eno. Suba looked at Eno and grinned.

"Together? " he asked.

"Together" Eno agreed.

"One, two... Three!" Suba and Eno both put the amulets on. Suba and Eno simultaneously yelled in pain. It was as if they were burning! But the fire suddenly went out and Suba was shocked. It was as if he had already learned magic and was just remembering it. Eno had the same experience. To test out his new abilities, Suba used the power of light and sent a ball of light hovering above them to light up the room. Not to be outdone, Eno grabbed his staff and sent a blanket of darkness over Suba's light. Suba had also picked up his staff. Suba asked "Sangun what do staffs do?"

"They can sometimes make you stronger but it would not work with you two. It also helps to tell others which power you are from though I think with you, you would like that to remain secret. So let me have your staffs as they are more hindrance than help to you" said Sangun. Suba and Eno gave them up without a grudge. "Ganuf could figure out that you command all powers. At least now you will have the element of surprise." For the first time Suba thought back to Fallou, Zimmo, and Brog. He asked "Sangun how are we going to find our friends?" Sangun answered with an expression of mock surprise on his face.

"Why, you didn't think that Sobask would leave you just like that now? Raguf will take you to him." Raguf smiled and said "ready to go on the path again?' Eno smiled mischievously and shook his head. One second later he disappeared. Suba got the gist and focused on the power to teleport but he didn't know what power to use. But it seemed as if he did not have to know which power. He teleported right outside the academy where Eno was standing. Eno was not too surprised to see Suba arrive. He laughed and said "do you think he will figure out what we did?" Suba also laughing shook his head. But at that very moment there was a small *pop* and Raguf appeared. But he was also smiling.

"So you are beginning to use your powers. Come I will show you Sobask." Suba turned and there right where he had dropped them stood Sobask. Suba and Eno ran toward him. Suba said to Sobask "it's good to see you."

"You too. Learned your magic?"

"Sobask, can you do magic?"

"Yes."

"Well can you teleport us to where the others are then?"

"Yes and before you ask yes I will." Suba told Eno to get on Sobask saying that he was going to teleport them to where the others were. They got on and Sobask teleported them. What Suba saw after that was amazing.

Chapter 15

The piece of land that they were on had lush green grass that was very soft. The whole island, for there was water on all sides of it, had not a single building on it. Suba looked to Sobask for an explanation. Before he could ask Sobask said *"you are wondering about your friends and this place? Do not looked so shocked. Almost everyone who sees it for the first time asks the question. This doesn't look like fun! But wish any place you want here and it will appear to your eyes only, unless you put a strong enchantment on it."* Suba wished for his house to appear and when he opened his eyes his house was right in front of him! He was about to run into it when Sobask caught him and told him to wait. Suba looked over at Eno and saw that the same thing had happened to him. What had Eno wished for Suba wondered? But he soon put that thought out of his mind because he had looked up and seen Fallou, Zimmo, and Brog. They were running towards him. Then Suba thought of a joke.

He barely turned his head or moved his lips but muttered to Eno so that Sobask couldn't hear "throw a blanket of darkness over yourself and disappear. The others will think that we are ghosts or a mirage or something." They both did at the exact same time. And while Suba could still see, no one could see him! Fallou, Zimmo, and Brog ran up out of breath and panting and Suba heard Zimmo say something to Sobask and Sobask answered, "they are right there. Can you not see them?" Zimmo and the others looked around. "Where" asked Zimmo. At that moment Suba and Eno made themselves visible. Fallou was so startled she let out a scream. Zimmo turned around and smiled while Brog who had been standing the closest jumped at least two feet in the air. Zimmo asked "how'd you do that? " and the next moment a gaggle of voices cascaded over them. Suba turned and cast a questioning glance at Eno. Eno nodded with a small smile and the next moment they had thrown their cloaks of darkness over themselves again. To make it a little more impressive, Suba added a burst of fire right in front of him. The others leaped back in alarm thinking Suba had been burnt. At last Suba nodded to where he thought Eno was and whispered "we'd best show ourselves to them now and quit disappearing. Come on!" Suba and Eno showed themselves. Zimmo jumped about a foot in the air. Fallou screamed. Brog, who was nearest to them, threw himself backwards yelling. Suba and Eno laughed. Pretty soon, Brog, Zimmo, and Fallou joined in. then Suba said "lets get back to that mountain and rattle Ganuf's bones!" They got on Sobask's back yelling war cries. Sobask smiled and teleported them. Once again, Suba thought how strange it was to have a dragon for a friend, right before Sobask teleported them. They arrived at the base of the fire mountain. There was a gaping hole in the side that Suba assumed Ganuf had blown open. No one seemed to want to do anything so Suba shook himself and said "well I guess we go in" and started walking forward. Brog raced past him yelling. Fallou, Eno, Zimmo, and Sobask followed Suba. Before he could call Brog back, a dark ball flew from above and struck Brog throwing him backwards. Suba immediately threw a cloak of darkness over him and the rest of the group but for some reason it didn't work. They watched in silence as Brog landed but got to his feet again. Ganuf dropped out of nowhere and put up his hand almost lazily. Suba saw that it was glowing with dark energy that Ganuf could form into a ball and throw at any second. Ganuf said with a sneer, "tell me. What were you planning to do?" Brog kept his lips sealed. Ganuf said "all right then. If that's the way you want it, fine." Ganuf's hand glowed brighter. Then Suba knew what he had to do. He focused his energy on the power of light and just as Ganuf hurled the ball Suba sent a shaft of light lancing towards him. The light and the dark ball met in mid air. Suba's light turned out to be stronger in the end and it cut through Ganuf's ball and went towards him. Shock showed on his face as the light went towards him as if in slow motion. It struck him in the chest and threw him back against the rocks of the mountain. As soon as his first shaft hit, Suba was out firing one after another at the spot where Ganuf had fallen until the rocks around him crumbled and fell. By now the others had gotten their senses back. Fallou jumped up and fired an arrow but it clattered harmlessly against the fallen rocks. Suba motioned for them to go in the hole. They were going in when Sobask said *"stop. I can teleport all of us to the place where the door is. I cannot teleport past it for it is made of an ancient magic. You shall have to figure out how to open it yourselves."* Suba, Fallou, Brog, Zimmo, and Eno climbed on Sobask who teleported them. This time though, Suba thought he could sense that Sobask's teleportation was not going very well. They seemed to be moving forward in bursts that gave them very painful tugs. When they finally got to the place that they were trying to get to Sobask said before anyone could so much as lift their heads

"I am sorry. The energies of the door were interfering with mine. That's why the ride was so bumpy." Suba sensed that they were in a room. When he lifted his head he saw a door in the rock side of the mountain. He could tell that they were very high up because of the narrowness of the room. Also, if he looked up he could see a light filtering down from the hole at the top of the mountain. Then he turned his attention to the door. It was a strange door that somehow gave of the appearance of power. It was blood red with spikes sticking up all over it. The were three gaps in the spikes. Wherever Suba looked he could find no means of opening the door aside from the three gaps in the door that gave no clue whatsoever like a handle or some sort of knob. When he looked close he saw that in the three gaps there were holes that went deep in the door which made Suba wonder how far it went. Then an idea hit him. He turned to ask Sobask about it but saw everyone else staring at the door dumbstruck. Suba went towards Sobask and asked "Sobask, you said we

would have to figure out how to get into the door by ourselves? Well I was wondering if you could answer a question." Sobask merely nodded in assent.

"Ok then I saw three gaps in the door where it seems three things might fit into. The gaps were in the shapes of circles. Would you know anything about this?"

"Alas I should have told you about the three keys. You need them to open the door. They are scattered throughout the land. I can take you to the general area of each yet pinpointing one and getting it would be your job. Of course as soon as you locate one I shall start helping you to get it. Get on." Suba told the others what Sobask had said.

"So we came all this way only to go back and look for three keys" said Brog.

"Yeah that doesn't seem fair" said Fallou. Zimmo said "well the sooner we start the sooner we end. Come on" the friends raced to Sobask and hopped on. Sobask teleported them and immediately the cold set in.

Chapter 16

The first thing that Suba saw was snow. The next thing he saw was a group of mountains with snowcapped peaks set in a circle as if to guard something. Sobask was lazily floating down towards those mountains. He breezed over the tip of one mountain and floated down into a valley. What Suba saw next shocked him. He had been looking over at Sobask's wings trying to imagine what it would be like to have such wings when he noticed that the air was no longer frigid and was becoming warmer. He heard Fallou gasp and a sharp intake of breath from Zimmo who was sitting behind him. He saw a lush green valley with trees and bushes sitting there. In the center of the valley there was a pool of water that had collected into a kind of basin formed by rock. The basin was circular and quite big. Big enough that all the Smaks could fit inside. It was towards this pool that Sobask headed after saying *"it appears you have been lucky. The first stone is in the center of the pool. As you can see it is not very deep but still be careful, that might not be the only thing guarding it."* Sobask did a roll in midair which dropped the Smaks. Suba felt himself falling but then slowing down all the way to a stop hovering far above the pool of water. Suba looked around and saw that the others were also hovering. Eno had a smug expression on his face and when he saw Suba looking at him he said "well I couldn't have our adventure ending already could I? I'll lower us to the water." "Hang on" said Suba thoughtfully.

"Didn't Sobask say something about other guards?" But Eno paid him no regard and started lowering everyone. Suba countered Eno's spell so he stayed there. Then he yelled for Eno to stop. But he kept going. Suba desperately focused his power on water and made the water in the pool blast up. Immediately, the biggest fish Suba had ever seen leaped up. It had a ball of some kind of energy gathered at its mouth. Suba realized just as the fish was about to release it that it was lightning. He had only a second to think as Eno was about to get zapped and eaten. He focused his powers on earth and from where he was in the air, sent a huge rock hurtling up from the ground into the lightning's path. The fish released its charged up energy. The lightning was flying towards Eno who stared at it dumbstruck. But then the rock Suba was commanding flew into the lightning's path and the lightning bounced off the rock. This did not matter to the fish as its earlier momentum carried it up towards Eno. Suba was sure it intended to gulp him down and sent the rock towards the huge fish. Caught by surprise the fish did not know what to do. The rock hit it head on and sent the fish flying towards the ground. By now everyone except Suba had landed on the ground. The fish was not moving but Suba knew he could take no chances. He eliminated the last of the energy holding him and dropped towards the ground which was a much faster way then how Eno, Fallou, Zimmo, and Brog had landed. Right before Suba crashed; he slowed himself down so that he managed to land on his feet. When he ran towards the fish, he saw that Eno and Fallou had already dealt with it. There were two arrows sticking out of it and it seemed like a kind of darkness hanging over it. Suba went to the lake where the others were standing. Eno who was looking down into the lake muttered "anyone here a good swimmer?" Brog smiled and jumped in. Fallou said "Brog it should be near the bottom. Remember we're looking for something in the shape of a circle. It could look like a pearl or, or anything." Brog dived under with a splash that wet them all. Zimmo idly stuck his spear in the water. As soon as he did it was almost tugged out of his grasp. Taken by surprise he was lifted off his feet and pulled towards the water. Fallou grabbed hold of his feet yelling for Suba and Eno to help. Eno grabbed hold of Fallou while Suba grabbed him. Together they formed a kind of chain that proved to be strong enough to pull Zimmo out of the water. As Zimmo slowly was pulled out, a pair of hands were revealed holding on to the spear with desperate energy. With a final tug, Zimmo, the spear, and the thing holding on to it were pulled completely out of the water. When Suba, Eno, and Fallou untangled themselves they saw Brog holding on to the spear with a fish clamped on to his leg. Fallou brought up her bow and fired. It had been impossible to miss at such close range. The fish went slack and stopped its wriggling. Brog opened his eyes and said something. Suba bent closer to ask what he had said, in reply all Brog did was slowly unclench one of his hands. There, sitting inside it, was a perfect sphere clear white, yet Suba thought that if he looked really deep inside, he could see a hint of green. Eno, Zimmo, and, Fallou crowded closer for a good look at the first key. Suba looked up at the sky while the others were examining the key. He thought he saw about five dragons flying high in the sky but he couldn't be sure. He fired a blast of white light straight up as Sobask had told him to do when they found the first key and retrieved it. Soon after, Suba heard the beat of wings that signaled Sobask coming near. The others heard it too. Sobask was in sight now and coming closer rapidly. Soon he was landing. He landed, and immediately demanded to see the key. Brog passed it to Suba who held it up to Sobask. It seemed to shine with an inner radiance thought Suba. He asked "Sobask, lets not waste anymore time. Can you get us to the second key?"

"Alas, how I am forgetting to tell you things. Focus your power on teleportation and hold the stone high above you. I will not come with you and if you make it focus your power on the last key and you will be brought here to the land of the Ice Key. Now go!" At that Suba held the Ice Key high and teleported the party letting the Ice Key lead him.

Chapter 17

Suba felt himself going down and farther down, never wavering in the split second of teleportation. They fell out onto a stone floor and when Suba examined this closely he realized that they were under the earth. When he pointed this out to the rest of the group, they looked at him with shocked faces.

"Well better start out then" said Zimmo lamely trying to break the silence. And that's what they did. Walk, walk, and walk some more. It seemed as if the road would never come to an end. At last Suba who was out ahead of the others called a rest. He was as tired as the rest of them and flopped down to get a rest. Soon though, Suba got up and started whispering to Eno. Eno nodded and smiled. Zimmo whispered to Brog "they are deciding something." Brog nodded and whispered back "probably deciding to keep us marching the rest of the night, or day. I can't tell one from the other in this infernal place." It seemed as if Brog's words would come to pass after all. Suba called them up to start walking again. There was a unanimous groan from the other friends, but they got to their feet anyways. None of the others noticed that Suba went to the front. But then this wasn't unusual as he always went to the front seeming to have tireless energy. What *was* unusual was that Eno went to the back. He usually walked just a bit behind Suba. After a while of walking with nothing whatsoever changing, everyone was tired. Even Suba full of energy like he was, seemed a little down. Eno smiled then lifted his head and shouted *move.* Suba responded by shouting back. Zimmo, Brog, and Fallou looked back from Eno to Suba wondering why they were shouting. All of a sudden Suba and Eno raised their hands which were glowing. Then Zimmo noticed that the ground beneath them was glowing.

"Guys?"

"Guys what's wrong with the groouuund!" The ground had began moving and taking them forward. Suba and Eno had lowered their hands and were standing on the glowing path smirking. They didn't have to walk anymore as the moving path took them forward. Soon everyone was laughing together happy that they no longer had to walk. At last, they came around a bend and found an amazing sight unfold in front of them. A city made entirely of mud bricks with some buildings much taller than the others. It seemed to go on for a long time until you could see a little mound rising up. There was nothing past that. Suba looked at it in surprise wondering who would build a city under the earth. For some reason he got the feeling that they shouldn't be seen. Eno seemed to have gotten the same feeling.

Eno quickly stopped the path. Suba threw a blanket of darkness over the whole group. Fallou and Zimmo seemed to know that there was a need to be quiet. But Brog exclaimed in wonder. "Isn't it wonderful? I mean imagine. A city under the earth. Who knows maybe a whole civilization?' Suba quickly threw a hand over Brog's mouth muttering "quiet. I don't think that we want to be heard." Suba raised his hands and soon everyone was hovering in the air with a blue outline. Then Suba sent them flying high over the city where they saw weird creatures walking in between the mud brick houses. They seemed to be balanced wrong considering the fact that their heads were twice as large as their body. Then one looked up and pointed at the group when they were about halfway to the mound. It moaned a low loud sound and soon a lot of the creatures were pointing up. Suba, who was already tired from the effort of flying the group the short distance that he had, abandoned all pretense yelled to the others "I put a cloak of darkness over us but they can see through it. This isn't good! Eno, throw some fire at them and see what happens." Eno obliged and threw some fire down in a curving arc. It was blasted out of the air with a blast of water. There was a group that was marching under them that seemed to be the army. It was huge, made up of at least fifty strong. There is no way that they could catch us thought Suba, and speeded them up. But the strange creatures seemed to be able to work magic too. They teleported to the top of the mound where Suba could see the second key held in a statues hand. But the creatures threw fire at them. Suba dropped them landing them roughly. Fallou had already got out her bow, but Suba told her to put it away.

"There is no way that we are going to fight every one of those creatures. But I have a plan. I'll put up a shield like I just did. I'll hold it for as long as I can." Suba shuddered as fire, water, earth, light, dark and ice hit his shield. "Eno, dig under those creatures grab the key come back here and teleport us out of here, go!" Suba's shield suddenly boosted its strength and Eno jumped, and disappeared into the ground. Suba couldn't hold on to his shield much longer, and Fallou, Zimmo, and Brog could tell. They kept on trying to encourage him to hold it. His eyes were closed as he fought the strain of the attacks keeping them from breaking through his shield. Fallou took out her bow and began firing arrows off into the crowd of creatures knocking them down. Zimmo drew Brog back a little ways, motioned to Suba who was now shaking on the ground fighting the attacks, and whispered "have you noticed him? He's holding out a shield against about fifty things at one time. I don't know any other wizard who's that strong." Brog nodded and then said "but you also don't know any wizards, and pointed, yelling "look, Eno got the key!" And indeed he had. He just grabbed it when the statue that was holding it came to life it raised a fist and knocked Eno flying. He waved his hand before he crashed into the ground and floated over behind Suba's shield. He raised his hand shouting that he had the key but turned around and realized that the creatures had gone. Zimmo pointed at the place were the statue had been, and it was standing up. It had opened its one eye when Fallou whispered Rock Golem. "I forgot how to defeat them!" Suba was lying on the ground in no condition to fight after holding up his shield for so long. Eno ran forward and bravely wrapped his mace around the Golem's feet. It roared and tried to take a step forward but tripped and fell. At that, Zimmo and Brog ran forward and jumped on top of the Golem. Zimmo was stabbing everywhere he could reach with his spear. Brog hacked at the Golem's neck with his axe. It lay still for a while in which time Eno was unwrapping his mace from the Golem's feet, when it kicked hitting it Eno hard and throwing him down the mountain. Zimmo and Brog were shaken from its back and thrown to the ground with their weapons still stuck in the Golem, while Fallou slowly retreated from it firing arrows. The Golem just kept punching the arrows away since his fists were made of rock like the rest of his body. Soon Fallou was at the place where Eno lay. She looked up into the Golem's one bloodshot eye that was glaring down at her. The Golem drew back its fist to punch her and then take the key since no one could stop it when Fallou remembered. The Golem's fist was coming towards her but she didn't pay any attention to it. She brought up her bow, took careful aim, and fired right before the fist smashed into her. The next moment a lot of things happened. Fallou's arrow went flying towards the Golem, the Golem's fist smashed Fallou down the mountain. The arrow that Fallou had shot went straight and true, and struck the Golem in the eye, right where Fallou had intended it to. The Golem let out a colossal roar, staggered back and forth, and looked down in surprise at the shaft of light protruding from his chest. Then the Golem fell. And behind him with his eyes blazing and light gathered at his hand. Stood Suba. Then he said quietly, but so everyone heard it, "don't dare to touch my friends."

Chapter 18

*Z*immo and Brog ran forward and took their weapons out of the dead Rock Golem. Suba slowly quieted down and went to help Eno. Fallou watched Suba go down to Eno and put his hands on Eno's chest. They glowed with a gentle blue light as Eno got up. Suba brought him back. Luckily Eno still had the second key clutched in his grasp after being knocked down by the Golem. Suba took it from him held it up and let it lead them to the next key. Suba noticed the darkness right away. How could he not when he couldn't see his hands in front of him? Then nearby a light flared. It was so bright that it also blinded Suba for a while. But then he could see clearly where they were. They were teetering at the top of a huge cliff which led down to a sea of lava. Suba was so surprised he let out a yell and jumped backwards as did Fallou who was also close to the edge of the cliff. Fallou turned and yelled "did you have to get so close?" Suba was also shaken up and said sorry to Fallou.

Zimmo, Brog, and Eno came over to see what the shouting was about and they were also surprised when they saw the sea of lava. Suba muttered to Eno "I'll bet you the next key is the fire key." Eno shook his head and went to look at the lava again. Suba looked after him then shook his head and asked for ideas. Eno turned back with a smile on his face and said "I have one. Come on!" Eno went to the very edge of the cliff and started to jump up and down. Suba ran forward to grab him before the cliff gave way and fell but it did give way before he got there. Eno fell, still smiling until the others saw him slow his flight. Then they heard him call up "come on down its safe. Suba you first. When you get down here we can make a net to catch the others." Suba agreed and started jumping up and down on another part of the cliff until it gave way. Then Suba fell down and slowed his flight when he heard Eno call. The mist that had been hovering at the top of the cliff was nowhere close to the bottom and Suba could see clearly. He looked to the left and saw Eno standing on the ledge that he was standing on. It circled the mountain completely. Eno was already weaving a net of magic when Suba landed. He got up to help and they finished very soon. They called up for the others to drop down and soon after Fallou came flying down immediately followed by Brog and Zimmo. Right after Zimmo got his feet safely on the ground, Suba turned to face Eno, his face pensive. Suba said to Eno "do you think that I could do some spell that would let me see very far? I don't know but I'm going to try it." And with that Suba made his eyes stronger with a spell and he could see out into the distance. When he turned a little bit to the right he saw an island. He turned to tell Eno. When he heard, Eno's eyes grew big. He said "but how are we going to get them up there" and jerked his thumb at Zimmo, Brog, and Fallou. Suba smiled and levitated himself in the air, and before Eno could say a thing, made them all levitate and start flying towards the island. Eno was shocked but he did not try to stop Suba. The others were yelling at him to stop but he wouldn't listen. Then, when they were about halfway there, giant fireballs started leaping up out of the sea of lava. Suba, who was levitating them, looked at Eno who raised his hands. Then Suba flew on, it seemed, without regard to the fireballs. Fallou could not take her eyes off of them. Whenever one came close, she would let out a scream. All of a sudden a big one leaped up right below them. Fallou let out a scream so loud if there had been any glass within a one mile radius, it would have shattered. Just when the fireball was about to hit them it stopped as it encountered Eno's shield. Eno shuddered visibly with the effort of stopping the fireball. By now they were almost at the island. Suba landed them setting them down in the black dust that covered the island saying "nice job there Eno. You held out against those fireballs really well. Especially that big one!" There were a lot of houses on the island, but when Brog went up to one and knocked he received no answer. The same thing happened with the next house and the next. Finally, Brog just pushed a door open. There was no one inside. But on a pedestal in the middle of the room stood the third and final key. The others rushed ahead right away to grab it, but Eno and Suba stood back. Eno whispered to Suba "don't you think that was a bit too easy?"

Chapter 19

Brog reached the pedestal first. He grabbed the key and held it in the air. At the moment Brog touched the key, a rope dropped down from the ceiling tying Zimmo, Brog, and Fallou together. They were yanked a little ways of the ground. The floor beneath them fell away to reveal a pit of lava. Suba noticed that the rope was thin and would not hold for long. He muttered this to Eno so low that the others would not hear. Eno nodded and yelled up to Zimmo "we will come back for you. We're going to try to find the real key and then come back for you once we have got it. Suba and Eno ran out side the house. Eno turned to ask Suba what he thought they should do, but before he could Suba said, "there are probably many more fake keys in the other houses. But the real key will probably be somewhere significant, with a guardian guarding it like the other two keys."

"Suba, wait. The rope holding the others was kind of thin, right? I think we should go try to help them first. I mean what if it breaks? It could take us a while to find the right house." Suba agreed and they ran back to what they thought was the house where the others were tied, except for that it was the wrong house. Then Eno realized with a stroke of despair that each house looked the same and wondered how they were going to find the house they had started out in. By some stroke of luck, Suba found them on the next house he tried. He yelled for Eno to come over and help him. Suba cast a spell that would bring them hovering down to safety except when it got close to them it seemed to bounce off an invisible wall. Suba ran forward except he also hit the wall. Suba picked himself off the ground and went up to the force field. He put his hands on it and tried to push through it. Then Eno appeared at the door. He saw what Suba was doing and said "here let me try. Stand back." Suba went a ways backwards. Eno raised his hand and fired ball after ball of dark energy at the shield. Except nothing seemed to be able to break through the force field. Suba thought for a while, and then decided that they should go try to find the real key. Then they could teleport everyone back to the place where they had found the first key and the place where Sobask would be waiting for them. They ran back out the door. Eno went one way, Suba went another. But Suba had noticed one thing that Eno had not. On the back wall of every house he had been into Suba had seen a 9 in a star. And on the front of the houses there were numbers. Suba checked in one more house to confirm his suspicions. There was also a number nine in a star at the back wall of that house too. Suba went out side and saw that the numbers were going down. He was at number thirty-eight. The house numbered nine is close to the end of this row thought Suba excitedly. He was about to call Eno, when he saw Eno come towards him from the end of the row of houses. Suba barreled towards him. In no time Eno was close. As soon as Suba could hear him, Eno yelled "have you found something?" Suba who was short on breath just grabbed Eno and panted "come on!" Eno was surprised but he ran following Suba. Suba got to number nine, tried to slow down, except was going so fast he tripped and fell. This of course made Eno who was coming up behind Suba fall because he tripped over Suba's feet. Suba by that time had gotten up and charged toward the door. He grabbed the handle and threw the door open. Eno had come behind Suba and looked over his shoulder. The room was plain and it looked just like all the other rooms they had been into. Except something was different. Not sight wise, but both Suba and Eno could feel another presence watching them to see what they're next move would be. The presence was full of malice like the room. It seemed as if the room itself did not want them to be there. Suba ran forward before Eno could say a word grabbed the key and started running back towards Eno. At that moment several things happened. A giant, flaming, well a *flaming giant* fell through the ceiling and pointed his fist at the spot where Suba had been standing just a second ago. The fire that shot from his fist burnt the wooden floor of the house and started a fire going. Suba dived forward and out of the house just as the giant shot the fire at him. He and Eno started running as fast as they could back to the house they thought was the house where the others were tied up. Before they had gone very far the fire giant leaped out of the house. Eno turned and noticed that the fire from the first house had made another house catch on fire. Eno realized that the houses were so close together that even one house on fire could get them all going. They ran up the next row as Eno told Suba what he had found out. All of a sudden Suba turned and tackled Eno. Eno got up ready to ask Suba why he had done that when he saw the smoking crater right where they had been standing. They got up and ran on every now and then having to dodge fireballs thrown by the giant. Then they heard a booming laugh. They kept on going but turned their heads to see what the giant was laughing about. The giant had thrust his hand high in the air and from it fireballs were erupting like a volcano. Several other houses in different rows caught fire. Just then Eno remembered seeing the number on the front of the house where the others were trapped. He grabbed Suba and turned him down a row where almost all the houses were on fire. Suba could barely get out enough breath to gasp out "Eno where are we going?" Eno just shook his head and kept on going. He skidded to a halt in front of a house that was half burnt and threatened to fall at any moment. Unluckily though, Eno's sudden halt sent Suba crashing into him which knocked them both to the ground. As they were getting up there was a gigantic crash that knocked them back to the ground again. Suba managed to get up quickly and pull Eno up beside him. But what they saw wasn't such good news. The fire giant had some how managed to find them again. And he was standing right before the door to the house where Zimmo, Brog, and Fallou were tied up! Suba whispered a hasty plan that he had thought up on the spot to Eno, who could see no better one on a split second, agreed. Suba charged to the right of the fire giant, while Eno charged to the left. They both shot streams of water as they ran, except Suba intensified his so much it was like several water cannons blasting. Suba who was on the right made the giant lean toward the left with his powerful blast of water. The giant, who was made of fire, hated the water. The giant tried to turn around, but had been pushed a little *too* far to the left. It teetered for a moment, and then as if in slow motion, fell.

Chapter 20

Suba and Eno raced around the giant. It was so big that it took it some time to get up. Suba, who held the Fire Key, got there the same time that Eno did. Eno looked up at the place where Zimmo, Brog, and Fallou were hanging, and then looked despairingly at Suba. He said "there is *no* way we are going to get past that shield that's guarding them. Or did you forget about that?" Suba shook his head for indeed he had not forgotten about the shield. He said "Eno, I think the key will allow us to go through the shield." Eno looked surprised for a moment, and then said with a shrug "lets try it. I mean, we have nothing to lose right?" Suba held the key firmly in front of him, and with Eno holding on, and Zimmo, Brog, and Fallou watching anxiously, took a deep breath and marched through the shield. When he managed to do that, Eno jumped up and cast the spell that would bring the others hovering down to where Suba and Eno stood. This time instead of bouncing off an invisible shield it worked as it was supposed to and brought the others down. Everyone grabbed hold of one another and just as Suba held the key high and was about to teleport them, the fire giant who had finally managed to get himself upright, fired a fireball at the remains of the house. The poor house could not contend with any more damage and went up in flames. It slowly began to crumble and then start folding in on itself. At that moment Suba's teleportation spell kicked in and began whisking them away. The last sight they saw was the fire giant roaring triumphantly for he had not seen them teleport. He believed he had gotten his prey. Suba felt a rush of emotions wash over him in that moment of teleportation, happiness, sadness, exhilaration, dread, and a sense of foreboding. The next moment they were hit with what seemed a wall of sunshine. After their time in the place where the Fire Key resided, the barest light would seem pretty bright. When they appeared, Suba heard a voice that he had been expecting never to hear again. Sobask.

"So you made it back. I must say I was expecting never to hear from you again. You got all the keys I take it?" Suba just nodded.

"Then what are we waiting for? Lets go open that door and get the flaming sword!" Suba hopped on Sobask's back motioning for the others to follow. Sobask teleported them without any further ado. When Suba opened his eyes, he saw the door looking the exact same as always in front of him. He ran forward with the keys while the others stood back apprehensively as if they expected something bad to happen. Suba was just about to put in the first key, when Sobask stopped him. *"Wait.*

I need a moment. I always wondered what was behind this door even when I was a hatchling. I suppose now I shall find out!" Suba put in the Ice Key followed by the Earth Key, and last but not least the Fire Key. The door began glowing. Then seemingly of its own accord, the door swung open. Suba called the others up to go through the door now that its brilliance had faded but Suba could tell that Eno was purposely trying to be the last one through. At the very moment that Brog was about step through it, there was a bang and Eno flew past them, hit a wall, and crumpled onto the floor. Suba saw the dark energy slowly fading and turned around with a sinking feeling and sure enough, there was Ganuf at the head of at least fifty Goven. His hand was sparking with dark energy. He smiled.

"Surprised to see me?" He fired another ball of dark energy at them that Suba countered with one of his own. Ganuf smiled and said "I see you've gotten better at magic. But can you take this?" He stuck his arm out and swung it in an arc. A wave of dark energy blasted out of it. Suba sent forward a flaming arc of fire to counter the dark. And with that same movement grabbed Eno and told the others to get in the gate. When Ganuf saw what they were doing he raised his hand and said something to the Govens. They charged forward, each one wielding a different type of weapon. Suba realized that he would not be able to fight all of the Goven without help from at least Eno. Brog, Fallou, and Zimmo had already gone through the door. Sobask just stuck his head in and disappeared. Suba was the only one left standing out with the Goven and Ganuf. He jumped in through the doorway. The last thing he heard was Ganuf shouting in anger. The room Suba appeared in was roughly circular and quite plain. The flaming sword was in a sphere of glass. At least Suba figured that it was the flaming sword because it was the only thing in the room. But it wasn't flaming. All of a sudden Goven started appearing. Suba yelled to Sobask "get the sword I'll get the others!" Sobask understood and let loose two bursts of fire, one at the Goven, and the other one at the sphere of glass. The Goven recoiled from the fire but began to gather themselves as more Goven appeared. The sphere of glass melted and Sobask grabbed the sword inside by hooking it with one of his claws. Suba sent Zimmo, Brog, and Fallou running towards Sobask. Then he magically threw Eno onto Sobask. The Goven had completely regrouped themselves by now and charged at Suba. He also threw himself magically over the heads of the Goven and landed on Sobask's back. Sobask teleported right out of the hands of several Goven. As they disappeared, Suba thought he saw Ganuf came through the doorway. They reappeared at the base of the fire mountain. Suba looked around for a minute then up and almost screamed. He turned to Sobask and asked him, well, more like yelled at him "WHY HERE! THEY ARE RIGHT UP INSIDE THAT MOUNTAIN AND WE BARELY MANAGE TO ESCAPE THEM AND YOU PUT US RIGHT AT THEIR FEET AGAIN!" Sobask urgently said *"calm down Suba. They can still hear you if you shout loud enough. I brought us here because Ganuf will have expected us to have gone as far away as we possibly could to hide the sword from him. He wouldn't think us stupid enough to stay anywhere close to him."* Suba considered this for a while and nodded but still told everyone to follow him as he led them into the shadows of the fire mountain where they could not be seen from anyone looking out from anywhere on the mountain unless they were not very high above them. Then he voiced the question they had all been thinking.

"If this really is the flaming sword, first of the mystical weapons, then how come it isn't flaming?"

Chapter 21

Sobask stared at Suba for a while before responding.

"I do not know. The only possible reason that I could think of was if someone took and hid the sacred gems. Suba, look at the sword. There should be five gems set into the hilt." Suba looked down at the golden hilt of the sword. There were indeed five spaces on the hilt where it looked as if gems could fit into. But Suba's gaze was drawn up to look over the sword before saying what he had found. The blade was extremely sharp and keen and the finest working Suba had ever seen. The hilt seemed as if it was made of pure gold. When Suba tried wielding it, the sword fit so well that it seemed like an extension of his arm. When he told Sobask and the others about the spaces on the hilt, Sobask hissed angrily and let out a puff of smoke. *"It is as I feared. The gems of power have been taken and hidden. Without them, the sword is merely a sword of very fine make. I know that this might be a shocking decision to you*

and you don't have to agree to it if you don't want to, but since there are five gems and five of you I think we should split up. It would make the going faster and that would give Ganuf less time to catch us with the sword. Every ten days or so we could meet back here to see how everyone is progressing. If some one does not return we could wait for one day and if they still don't return we would know that they were most probably captured by Ganuf." Suba, Eno, Zimmo, Brog, and Fallou looked up at Sobask in amazement. It was the longest speech he had ever given. Suba was indeed shocked by Sobask's decision as were the others. They had been together from the very start of the journey and had not split up. But Suba could see the sense in Sobask's plan. He knew that they needed to hurry. Suba said "all right lets take a vote. All in favor of splitting up say yes." Suba, Fallou, and Zimmo said yes, while Eno and Brog said no. So it was then decided that the friends would split up each looking for a different gem and meet back where they were every ten days. Suba would look for the Emerald. Eno, the Diamond, Zimmo, the Sapphire, Fallou, the Topaz, and Brog the Ruby. Sobask said he would wait here for all of them to come back. Another thing that he mentioned to the Smaks was that if they found their gem they should come straight back here. Sobask stood them up then, each facing a different direction and teleported all of them to look for their gem.

Chapter 22
Suba

Suba felt Sobask teleport them. When he opened his eyes after the teleportation he saw that he was on a grassy plain that seemed to go on forever. He didn't wonder for long about where the others had gone, because in the distance he saw a rising cloud of dust. He decided to wait for the dust cloud to reach him for he knew that only some riders would have kicked up that much dust. Considering how far away the dust was Suba reasoned that it would take some time for the riders to reach him. He was very tired from the events that had happened and thought that he could take a short rest before the riders reached him. The next thing Suba knew was that the ground was rocking and rolling beneath him. He reached down and felt something soft and furry. He cracked his eyes open and looked down. He saw a horse. Suba tried to jump up except he was tied by his hands and his feet to the horse. Then he tried to cut himself free of his bonds. But all his efforts came to nothing in the end. Suba resigned himself to the fact that he was not going to get through the rope holding him. Whoever had tied him on had known how to tie ropes. Suba looked around him and to the left he saw a rider completely swathed in cloth. Another rider was on the right. When Suba looked around he saw that there were many, many riders completely boxing him in. Soon the riders stopped, for night was falling. Suba thought that he would be able to get away during the night without being noticed but if he was he would fight his way out of the camp. Suba was put inside a tent by another rider who was covered in cloth. Suba lay on the ground and tried to calm his breathing as he looked around. He could see two stationary shadows against the side of the tent. Suba wondered at this and reasoned that prisoners must be highly valued to these people if they even put guards around them. Suba was still quietly trying to get free from the ropes binding him when a thought came to him. He could use magic! Suba would have slapped himself on the forehead if he could. He just wasn't getting used to the new idea of having magic at his fingertips. He burnt through his bonds but not before casting some darkness around him so the guards would not see the glow from the small fire. Suba then thought about how he would get out without making much of a fuss. He thought about throwing a cloak of darkness around him and just walking out of the camp. He thought that was the best idea he was going to come up with since it only had a few small risks like that he would trip over something or let out a noise. Suba was about to throw the darkness over him when he thought of a better plan. He could tunnel out. He was about to do that when he heard the tent flap opening. With that he had to lay flat out and pretend that he was sleeping. After a while it seemed that the person believed him to be sleeping because he left the tent. Suba got up, put up a soundproof barrier between him and the guards to make sure that they would not hear him tunneling out of the tent, and began to tunnel. It went much faster then Suba had expected. Soon he reasoned that he was halfway across and decided to peek up to see where he was. Suba stuck his head out of a hole and cautiously looked around. What he saw surprised him. The camp that he had left was very far away. He jumped out of the hole and looked the other way which was a mistake because he was standing right next to a cliff! Suba scrambled backwards from the thin ledge he was on but not before he got a look at what was at the bottom of the cliff. At the base of the cliff there were huts and what looked like a small village was formed. But that was not the most surprising thing about the village. It was that the whole village was on the shore of the sea of lava that Suba had crossed when trying to find the third key! And the strangest thing was that the people who were walking up and down in between the huts seemed not to notice or care that there was a sea of lava right next to them! Suba sat down to give this new development some thought. He reasoned that the people who had captured him where probably going to the village. And Suba felt that he should cross the sea of lava again. So the only thing that he could do was to get by the village and across the lava. With this in mind, Suba started sliding down the cliff.

Chapter 23
Eno

*E*no found himself at the base of a gigantic mountain that went so high it passed the clouds. It seemed to go on into infinity and Eno knew that he would have no chance to climb to the top, but he started climbing anyway seeing as he had nothing better to do. Eno had been climbing for quite a while and was getting tired when he spotted a ledge above him that would be an ideal place to rest. Eno climbed up but was stopped just short of his goal because he could not find any handholds taking him higher up. Stymied he tried to reach back to the last foothold with his foot but found that he could not reach that either. He was stuck. Eno knew he could not hold on for a lot longer and was about to call for help when he realized that something with a furry face was on the ledge was peering down at him. He was muttering something under his breath that sounded suspiciously like they always get themselves stuck there. Then turning around it called out "well it seems we have a visitor. Not that we get many up here. Though whenever we do get one they get themselves stuck there. I've seen it happen many times. Well if you're friendly I suppose I better help you though if you're here to harm or eat me I suppose I'll just leave you there." The creature looked inquiringly at Eno who said "no sir I'm not here to harm you except I don't need any help." Eno levitated himself off the cliff with magic and brought himself up to the little ledge. The little creature was staring at him wide eyed and said "I've seen many of them get stuck there but none of them ever did that. No chance!" when Eno got a chance to look at the little creature up close he realized that it wasn't very big at all, quite small in fact. His whole body was covered in a brownish fur. When Eno looked around he was amazed at what he saw. The ledge that had looked small from underneath was enormous. There was a small farm with a cave in the back. While Eno was standing slack jawed in amazement, the little creature went to the cave and called out "Diggety, Ruffler, come on out we have a visitor!" Eno walked over to the cave very carefully as he was trying not to step on any part of the garden. Diggety and Ruffler turned out to be the little creatures' family. His name was Kanak and he and his family lived way up in the mountains. This was just their home when they wanted a change or if they were forced to move. This time they had come just for a change in the scenery explained Kanak hurriedly when he saw the worried expression on Eno's face. Diggety, Kanak's wife asked him to stay for dinner. Eno graciously accepted the offer because he knew that he would offend the little family's feelings if he declined. And anyways, he was hungry and tired after his long climb. He followed them in and saw that the table was already set. Diggety went and found another chair for him, and put a plate of food in front of him. Ruffler, their little son stared at Eno in amazement. Soon he said "you must have eaten a lot to get that big huh?" Diggety leaned over and told Ruffler not to bother their guest but Eno shook his head and told Diggety that he didn't mind answering his questions. Eno said "yep I sure at a lot when I was your age. Its what made me big and strong." Ruffler stared in awe. After dinner, it was getting dark out and Eno knew he would not be able to resume his climb without running a high risk of falling. So it was decided that he would stay overnight and get an early start in the morning. Kanak lit his pipe and leaned back in a big plush armchair clearly wanting to talk. Eno decided to break the silence first. He said "I suppose that you want to know my story about how I came to be climbing one of the highest mountains in the land. Well it's quite long but if you are really prepared to listen, settle yourself. It's a long story." So Eno told the little family about his travels with his friends, being chased by Goven and Ganuf, finding the sword and barely escaping with it, getting magical powers, and separating, each going after a gem to power up the sword. He told them that he was looking for the diamond and that when Sobask had teleported them this was where he ended up. He told them that they were supposed to make their way back to the place that they had started from in ten days. Then he asked them if they had heard of a diamond somewhere on the mountain or close to it. Kanak and Diggety exchanged a worried glance. Then Kanak got up and said "there is such a jewel. It resides on the very tip of this mountain. You could try to climb up there except you would never make it all the way. I can show a secret passage known only to us that will get you within sight of the summit. Except I cannot come with you. There is a very fierce tribe that lives up there. Some say that they pray to the diamond. As the legend goes, the diamond streaked across the sky and in a bright flash came to rest way up high on the top of the mountain. Many before you have tried to go up except almost every one fell back down for as the legend goes, there is a part of the mountain when you are getting close to the diamond that is enchanted." Here Kanak's face flickered strangely in the firelight. "It surrounds the whole mountain except for one small part that is to steep and has too many rock falls so you cannot go by it. It is said that at that place you will fall asleep no matter how strong or awake you are. And when you fall asleep you lose your grip and plummet down the mountain."

Chapter 24
Zimmo

Zimmo found himself in a forest after getting teleported. He looked around but could see nothing that gave him a clue as to where he was. There was nothing much to do so he started walking. Soon after he started he stopped to look around thinking that he did not like the feel of the forest. It was too dark, too dense. Who knew what secrets it could hide? Zimmo took out his spear and started walking warily. Soon he was sure that there was something uncanny about the forest, something profoundly wrong. He broke into a run looking all around unfortunately for him, he was not looking down and he ran right into a trap that had been well disguised by leaves and branches woven together very carefully. He stepped on the branches and they gave way. He fell down a pit almost landing with his leg twisted under him. After a bit he got up and looked around. The pit was pretty deep and the walls of it were very smooth so Zimmo did not think that he would be able to climb out. Zimmo gauged the hole to be a little bit out of his reach even when he jumped with his arms stretched above him. After a while Zimmo began to get hungry and started to think that if something or someone did not come by soon, he would die. Lucky for him something did come by, except it was not anything like Zimmo had expected. A porcupine came by. Except this porcupine was not normal. It could talk. At first, Zimmo thought that he had gone delirious. Then he realized after the porcupine went away and came back that he probably wasn't. The porcupine said "well, well, well. What do we have here? Osman needs to see this." With that the little porcupine marched away. Zimmo almost went crazy. Soon though, the porcupine came back. "Well what did I tell you Osman? Is this strange or what?" The porcupine's head could be seen by Zimmo if he looked up. Its head was thrust out of the way by a massive paw and a bear's head came into view. The bear muttered and murmured to itself for a while then withdrew its head. Then he came back and talked it seemed to Zimmo. "We have not seen Smaks in this forest since long ago when it became protected by magic spells and such. I do not know how you managed to penetrate the magical spells and I am not sure that we should let you out of our trap." Zimmo's mind was racing furiously with the idea of talking civilized animals who knew how to build traps. The only answer he came up with was that he was seeing things or dreaming. In an effort to find out if any of this was real Zimmo pinched himself rather hard. He yelped. It hurt and that meant that he was probably still awake unless it was magic or his own mind trying to fool him. The bear continued.

"Maybe we should just let you rot here in our trap. Yet I am most curious to find out the means you used to penetrate inside our forest. I can see that you will most likely have a long tale to tell. Know that all animals here trust each other and lying is not tolerated. If you lie, we will know and never trust you again. I will call a gathering of all the animals to help me decide what to do with you. And if to many animals vote against you, well then I would not like to be in your position at the moment." The bear dropped some food down to Zimmo which he fell upon eating ravenously. After that the bear left and as Zimmo had nothing much to do, he thought that he might as well try to get some sleep. But it was hard to go to sleep in such a confined area. It was so small that Zimmo could not lie down even halfway and was forced to try to sleep standing up. It took a while but he managed to do it. In the morning he woke up and found himself almost starving again. His stomach felt like a bottomless pit which no amount of food could ever fill. The porcupine that had first seen Zimmo yesterday came back soon and pushed some food down to Zimmo and stood watching him eat it. After he was done the porcupine stared at him curiously for a few minutes then left. After another while Zimmo fell asleep as there was nothing better that he could do and it seemed that he would need his strength to face this council that Osman, whom Zimmo presumed was the bear, was talking about. Zimmo was rudely awakened later by a parrot pecking him. It said "the council wishes to see you."

Chapter 25
Fallou

Fallou opened her eyes after the teleportation to find herself on a warm sandy beach. Fallou had always loved beaches when she was little because she got to play in the water. Fallou looked down the coast and in surprise saw that it continued as far as her eyes could see. She looked on the other side and the same phenomenon repeated itself. She turned away from the water and found cliffs that she would not be able to climb. She looked forward and saw the water again. It seemed that the only way that she could go was into the water. But how she thought. I can't breath underwater. If only Suba or Eno were here. They could probably use their magic to let me breath underwater. Well they're not here and it looks like I'm just going to have to find some way to do it myself. Fallou got up from where she lay in the sand and began walking looking out for anything that might help her to breathe underwater. First she collected all the shells that she could find thinking with some crazy inspiration that she would be able to build a shell helmet that would let her breath underwater. She quickly threw out that idea after realized that she could not build a shell helmet and that it would probably not let her breath underwater. After a bit longer Fallou sat down on the beach again thinking that the whole thing was pointless. She yelled "this is hopeless! Why couldn't have someone else gotten this job?" at that point after the final echoes of her cries had stopped she spotted something shining in the water. At first she did not think that it would be worth anything if she looked at what it was. But eventually curiosity overcame her and she got up and decided to go and have a look at whatever was making the shine in the water. When she saw what it was at last it took her breath away. It was exactly what she was looking for! A submersible, half buried lay in the sand! Fallou didn't even give one single thought to the fact that the ship was buried halfway and that it would take a lot of her strength to get it all the way out. Finally as night was falling, Fallou gave one final yank to the ship and tugged it free of the sand. Fallou fell backwards onto the sand with the force of her pull. She got up and watched anxiously to see if the old rusty ship would float. Lucky enough for her it did. Fallou spotted a place that looked as if you were supposed to get in from on top of the sub. Fallou climbed on top of it. The sub bobbed in the water but still floated. Fallou turned a wheel on the door or hatch as Fallou would later find out and it opened. Fallou dropped inside closing the hatch behind her. The sub was not too roomy inside but at the same time it was not too confined. There was a set of controls set in paneling at the front of the sub. Fallou only found out the meaning of some of them. Luckily she found the steering controls and the way it sunk underwater and rose back up. Fallou had a feeling that the topaz that she was after would be hidden somewhere underwater. She gave the control for the sub to start sinking slowly and it obeyed her. The wall in front of her was completely made of glass to help Fallou see where she was going. Fallou gave the command for the ship to go forward before she looked down and realized just how vast a place she was in. it was so deep that even Fallou with her keen eyesight could not see the bottom. She stopped going forward and let the sub sink for a while. After this went on for almost thirty minutes Fallou began to become scared thinking that she would never reach the bottom. She was about to pull the sub back up and try again later when she saw something tall and pointed rising up from the deep. She got excited and made the sub start going down even faster. Soon the rest of the wreck of a sunken ship was revealed. What Fallou had seen was the mast rising high above the rest of the ship. In about a minute Fallou had made a complete circle of the ship and found a hole that was big enough for the sub to get into. Fallou hoped that it did not narrow as it went along for the sub was too big and unwieldy for small narrow places. Soon Fallou was near the hole and about to go in when she realized that the hole was glowing slightly blue from the inside. Curious, but also cautious, Fallou drifted closer trying in vain not to be seen. What she saw was so amazing that Fallou just stood at the controls for almost a full minute before moving again. The hole below her was full of weird alien octopus creatures. They all had a glowing blue power source inside of them and they were fully armed for battle it seemed. They each carried what could have passed for a regular lance or spear except for the fact that they glowed bright blue at the point and Fallou was sure that if you were struck by one of them that it would not feel like a regular lance or spear point. All of a sudden the creatures started streaming out of the hole glowing blue with their lances held above them. Their shapes were smooth and streamlined and Fallou knew that the sub would never be able to rise fast enough to escape them. So Fallou ran from the controls looking around for something, anything that would help her to evade the creatures. As she ran about, Fallou's leg accidentally kicked against a portion of the wall which opened showing her a suit for breathing in water. Fallou frantically put it on, went to the controls, smashed all the buttons, went to the hatch and went in the water.

Chapter 26
Brog

Brog opened his eyes to find glaring whiteness on all sides. It blinded him. When he finally managed to open his eyes again, he found that he could see much better and the glare was reduced. He managed to take a better stock of his surroundings. What he saw was ice. Ice was everywhere and that was all that there was to see. Brog looked in all directions but it was the same every which way he looked. Then he realized that he was standing on top of a medium-sized hill. A crafty idea came to him. He took out his shield and set it at rest on the ice it started sliding. Brog jumped on shouting happily. When he was about halfway down the hill, Brog realized that he was going much to fast and that his speed would double by the time he reached the bottom of the hill. Brog tried to think up an idea that would save him except none came. By now, he was three quarters the way down the hill and going so fast that his skin was being pulled backwards. Then an idea came to him brought out of sheer panic. He managed to drag his axe in front of him. He thought that if he did not manage to do something soon, the flesh would be stripped from his body. He threw his axe behind his head and managed to hold on to it as it lightly dug into the ice. The next second it was almost torn from his grip as the shield shot downward. Then, at that moment, a terrible realization hit Brog. What he had taken to be the bottom of the hill was merely an ice shelf that went completely around the hill. Mountain, not hill thought Brog as he realized that the hill so far was only one-fourth of the way down the complete mountain. Brog grimly clung onto his axe as he neared the shelf. Brog knew that it was slowing his process as it dug into the ice behind them. But there was one factor that Brog had not calculated. The ledge would give him a little bump. And at the speed that he was going, it would probably throw him of the face of the mountain altogether! The ledge was just a few seconds away, and Brog was clinging to his axe for dear life. Then everything changed. Brog's shield hit the ledge and Brog, on his shield was flung out into the air. Brog involuntarily let go of his axe which flew into the air. Brog's position was that his shield was now dropping straight downward, he had lost his axe, and that he had no way whatsoever to slow himself down. But Brog got lucky it seemed for his axe dropped right into his lap and the mountain got wider the lower you went so that he would eventually hit the side of the mountain again. Now if Brog had gone down the other side of the mountain he would have met Eno climbing to get to the top of the mountain. For that matter, if Eno had started into the forest he would have meet Zimmo in the forest. And if Zimmo had started walking in the other direction when he was teleported into the forest, he would soon have come to the top of the cliffs that Fallou had seen from the water. And if Fallou had started out in the submersible she soon would have come upon the sea of lava, headed to the coast, and have seen the village and Suba sliding down the hill. But none of this ever happened and each Smak went different ways. So Brog now had his axe again and his shield had just hit the mountain about halfway down with considerable less speed than it had before. But that soon changed as the shield sped up again. Brog used his old trick of sticking his axe into the ice behind him to slow him down. It did help some, but despite his efforts, his shield continued to speed up. Brog was three quarters the way down the mountain when his skin started to peel back again. Then a weird, half-formed idea came to Brog. He sat for about five seconds thinking it out fully before he realized that it would probably work. His skin was ripping back now, but Brog, with a tremendous effort, managed to bring his axe back to his lap. The next thing Brog realized was that his shield was going to hit level ground not a gentle sloping hill the would make him slowly lose the shield's speed. This made him make a few modifications to his plan which cost him another precious few seconds. Brog had realized that if he did not get of his shield by the time it reached the bottom of the mountain, he would be flattened. By now he was about three seconds away from crashing. Brog threw out his axe and forced himself to jump off his shield. His axe had embedded itself in the ice and Brog was hanging by his axe's handle not to far off the ground.

Chapter 27
Suba

Suba reached the bottom of the cliff as night fell. The shower of pebbles and rocks that followed him down frightened Suba for he feared that they would wake the villagers who lived in the huts. But none of the villagers woke or came out to get him. He thought that he would get over the sea of lava again by levitating himself across. So he levitated himself up and went moving in a forward direction. Soon he flew over the villages. No one or thing saw him except for a baby in a cradle that was hanging outside his hut from a pole. But Suba didn't think that he would say anything. And even if he did, they would have a tough time catching him as he flew over a sea of lava. Suba looked forward in the dull dreariness as he flew, his eyes trying to pick out the island. At long last he saw it. By now Suba had almost fallen asleep several times, which would have resulted in him crashing down into the lava and being burnt alive. Just as

Suba had begun celebrating, he seemed to hit a magic wall that would not let him levitate past it. Suba tumbled straight towards the sea of lava. The only things that saved Suba from a horrible fiery demise was some incredibly quick thinking and a bit of magic. He made a ball of earth that was as large as a room and put himself inside. The earth hit the fire and sank, but did not burn. Suba knew that plain old earth would not have held out too long against the fire so he had put some water into the earth. So if the fire did manage to burn through the outer earth, the water in the room's inner walls would be sufficient to stop it cold for hours if not days. Of course Suba did not plan to spend days or in fact, even hours in the little room. He got to work right away and made one whole wall of his room transparent so that he could look at it and see outside. The next thing he did was to put the ball of earth floating up to the surface. Surprisingly, he found that he was not very far away from the island by looking through the transparent side of the earth. Suba thought for a while on how to get the ball closer to the island for the lava seemed to be carrying him away from it. Then he made the lava flow change direction. Now it was carrying him *towards* the island. After a while the ball of earth was almost at the island with no mishap or hindrance happening to Suba who was very glad thinking that he had had enough excitement for one day. He took a little nap expecting to be woken up when he reached the island. But as soon as he closed his eyes it seemed, he was rudely shaken awake. The ball of earth was rocking madly. Suba yelled in surprise as he saw a *lava fish* jump out of the lava and crash against the transparent side of his little ball of earth. The earth spouted a leak of lava right where the fish had struck. Soon, more leaks appeared from more fish it seemed and the ball of earth was quickly filling up with lava. Suba managed to climb onto the ceiling of it and hang on. But the lava would soon reach him and he would have nowhere to go. But then Suba felt something that felt like one of the most welcome things in the world. He had felt the little ball of earth bumping against the island. Suba looked out the transparent side and sure enough, he saw the island. Suba blasted open a path through the thin layer of mud that was left by shooting balls of darkness at it. He jumped out on the island just as the entire ball began to sink. Suba was just thinking that he should have looked at the sights more closely because it's not everyday that you get to ride in a ball of mud and dirt in a sea of lava. But he was surprised when there was a sudden explosion of heat behind him that rocked the earth he was standing on. Suba fell on his knees on the ground. Slowly he got up and turned around. There, right where Suba had been standing not to long ago, was a fountain of fire blasting up from inside the earth. Suba went around it only to be shaken to his knees again by several more of the explosions. Suba looked up and saw that there were several other fountains of fire blasting up out of the earth in front of and behind him. Suba, as he stared around in growing horror, realized that he was standing in a field of fire geysers!

Chapter 28
Eno

*K*anak got up and said "time for bed. We have a long way to walk and we will have to get up early in the morning. While we are walking in the passageway I will answer any questions that you might have. Though I warn you. I most probably will not be able to answer all your questions. Now time for you to go to bed." Eno got into the bed without complaint but stayed up for a long time afterwards not being able to sleep. He kept on running his mind over what Kanak had said about the diamond at the top of the mountain and the fierce tribe who lived there and the secret passageway that Kanak was going to show him. He wondered how he would be able to get the diamond, get back into the secret passageway, and down the mountain without getting caught by the tribe. Finally, when the night was halfway through, Eno managed to get some sleep. For Eno, it seemed as if he had just closed his eyes when he was shaken awake by Kanak. Quietly, he motioned for Eno to follow him. When they were far from the little cave but still on the ledge, Eno asked Kanak why he had wanted him to be quiet. Kanak said "I didn't want to wake my wife and son." They trekked on in silence for some time. Then Eno saw a little hole cut into the side of the cliff. Eno asked if they were going to be going through the hole. Kanak responded with a grunted yes. Eno had some doubts if he would be able to fit in the hole but he did not voice them out loud. Of course Kanak, being smaller than Eno, should be able to fit through quite easily. But Eno was a lot bigger than Kanak and might not be able to get through. They reached the hole and Kanak slipped right in. Eno tried to go in right after him and also tried to make sure that his face did not show that he was almost frightened out of his wits. He stuck his arms through and then tried to fit his body through. He made it halfway, but then got stuck. He could not move forward or backward no matter how much he pulled, tugged, twisted, or turned. Finally he gave and called for Kanak. Since he had his eyes closed, he did not realize that Kanak was right next to him. He shouted as loud as he could for Kanak and nearly knocked out his eardrums. Kanak poked Eno, rather hard, on top of his head to make him stop. Eno quit and felt his arms, which were already through the hole, being grasped and pulled by Kanak. But even with their combined efforts, they made little headway. As they went up for one final tug, Kanak was pulling as hard as he could while Eno wiggled furiously trying to get free, Kanak slipped on the floor and went into the air landing on his back. That was the final tug that Eno needed to get free. As he tried to flip over, Kanak's tug came and Eno flew out of the hole landing on top of Kanak who was lying dazed on the floor. By now Kanak was sorely bruised and told Eno about every little ache that he had. After a while Eno helped Kanak get up and paused staring in shock at their surroundings. For the cave's walls were made up of crystal!

Chapter 29
Zimmo

The little bird led Zimmo through the forest frequently stopping on trees to let Zimmo catch up to it. It was a winding path that took a long time and made Zimmo lose almost all the strength that he had been saving up from his resting in the pit. The path if you could call it that, took almost three hours. And it was made worse for Zimmo, not only because of his growing fatigue, but also because of the bird who kept sniping at him any insult it could think of it seemed. First and most commonly he berated Zimmo for being so slow. Then he would start taunting him about being stuck to the ground and not being able to fly. At long last, after three long hours that had seemed like years to Zimmo they reached the council. The bird stopped before a clearing of trees and motioned for Zimmo to go in. There was Osman sitting on a chair and a few other chairs were set next to his. The rest of the animals who were just watching the trial were sitting on the ground behind Zimmo. Many of these animals had never seen a Smak before. So he did not blame them for staring at him curiously and holding up their children so that they could get a better look. Soon Osman raised his voice and called for silence. "You all know why we are here today. A Smak, a creature that we have not seen since the great change when spells were laid on our forest to stop intruders from coming in. this rises several questions. How did this Smak get in? Does he have magical powers? Are there more of them coming? I suggest that we should hear this Smak's story before we make a decision. Please tell us your story." At this Osman folded his paws and stared pointedly at Zimmo. Zimmo started to tell his story about how he had got there very slowly and hesitantly. He said "please my name is Zimmo. And if you really want me to tell you how I got here, settle in, because it will take a while."

Chapter 30
Fallou

Fallou flew out of the hatch like a rocket. The suit that she had put on had little rocket boosters that worked only under water. The blue octopus creatures flew on straight towards the ship not realizing that its only passenger, Fallou had escaped. The front one raised his lance high and bashed it through the glass of the sub. At that moment several things happened. The whole sub crackled with electricity. The controls that Fallou had smashed came into action and blew up the sub. The front creature was ultimately destroyed. The blast from the explosion hurtled through the water killing several more of the blue creatures. Fallou who had been swimming as fast as she could towards the wreck of the ship that the blue creatures had come out of, was just taken over by the blast and was flung forwards straight at the wreck headfirst. Luckily for her, the blast was so huge that it blew apart the ship. Fallou had forgotten that there were many, many more of the blue creatures in the ship. Since the blast had traveled some way before reaching Fallou and the other creatures, they were just dazed not killed by it. The creatures streaked out of the ship heading towards the thing that had given them such a blast. This time every single one of them went up towards the sub holding high their blue lances. As soon as one managed to hit it with its lance, the whole thing crackled with blue electricity and shot out several beams of electricity killing more of the blue creatures. But there were so many of them that it did not make much difference at all to their numbers. But this was all the distraction that Fallou, who had just recovered from being dazed since she had been closer to the blast than all the other creatures, needed to head straight for the ship and rocket into the hole that the creatures would normally have occupied. As she went in the hole, she looked around her and found that the walls of the ship were glowing blue. Fallou knew that she did not have much time to get in and out of the ship because the creatures would soon get tired of their game of playing with the sub. If that happened before Fallou got out she would either have to wait for something to disturb the creatures again which could take a long time, try to search for any other opening that would let her out of the ship, or just wait till all the oxygen ran out in her tank of oxygen. Fallou went forward propelled by her rocket boosters which she turned on again. The old ship creaked even underwater and Fallou turned at every one of them expecting to see the creatures streaming back in. Fallou went through a hole on the inside of the ship into the next room. There was a small door at the end of the room that Fallou was almost certain that led to the captain's quarters. She tried the door but found it locked. She thought for a while and got an idea. She went backwards till she was almost back in the other room, lowered her head so that the helmeted part was facing directly forward. Then she opened her rocket boosters to their maximum power and charged straight forward cutting through the water like a silvery arrow. She bashed through the door of the room, startling five of the creatures that had been sitting inside. But just as one creature wrapped a tentacle around her leg she spotted a glittering topaz gleaming on the captain's desk.

Chapter 31
Brog

Brog took stock of his situation. He was hanging by the handle of his battleaxe on the side of a mountain made completely of ice and snow. His shield was about to crash into the ground going at a tremendous speed. He craned his neck around and watched his shield crash down into the ice at the bottom of the mountain. Since Brog was only hanging about a few feet off the ground, he wiggled his axe free of the ice and jumped down. The sharp edge of his shield had cut deep into the ice, almost half of it was buried in the ice. Brog hefted his axe and chopped at the ice around his shield because he knew that he would not be able to pull his shield out of the ice because it was to deeply embedded. Soon after a bit more chopping, he managed to pull his shield free. He got up from where he sat on the ice, and looked around. What he saw startled him. Several giant beings, seemingly made of ice themselves, were standing on the ice next to Brog. He got out his axe and held in front of him even though he did not know if they were enemies or not. But that changed when one of the giants raised a huge fist and punched the spot where Brog had been standing. The only thing that had saved Brog was the giant's slowness. He didn't think that he or his shield could have held out against such a mighty blow as the one of the giant's fist. The ice where he had struck was cracked badly. Brog raised his axe and shield and charged the giants. He ran between ones legs hacking at them. The only problem was that they didn't seem to leave a lot of damage. Then he realized that little white specks were flying out wherever he hit one of the three giants. The next thing he realized that they were flecks of ice! To late he remembered stories of ice giants and their breath that can freeze you solid. He looked up right at one of the ice giants to find that it was blowing on him! He held up his shield. The giants' breath covered his shield and then solidified into ice. Brog stared at his shield in horror, then quickly flung it to the ground. He threw himself into a dive, landed on the ground, rolled over, jumped up and slashed wildly with his axe. Lucky for Brog as he flailed he hit the ice giant's weak spot. He chopped the first ice giant at his knee and the giant went down on one knee. The other two giants stood watching impassively. Brog looked at the giant quizzically and then had an idea come to him. He raised his axe and brought it down on the giant's other knee. The giant wailed a long, bone-chilling cry, and shattered into several ice shards that flew about. Brog dived for his frozen shield and held it up hearing several ice shards strike and crack against it. Brog turned to face the other giants with renewed hope and ferocity. He raised his axe and chopped one of the giant's knees before they could respond being big and slow. He raised his axe, chopped triumphantly at the giants other knee and turned around to deal with the other giant. But he had forgot about their breath. He turned and found the other giant blowing on him!

Chapter 32
Suba

*S*uba stared in shock. *A whole field of these geysers I can see! There's no chance of a way around them. They go as far as I can see* thought Suba. Suba squared his shoulders and started marching resolutely forward, only to be stopped in his tracks by a red-hot geyser blasting up right where he was going to step. Suba stumbled backwards and almost fell straight into another geyser that would have burned him alive. He let out a yell of surprise and threw himself to his knees while geysers blasted up in front of and behind him. Suba sat and thought that there was no chance for him to get across unprotected. Suba looked up to see the geysers tops not going all that high up. Of course it was about as tall as four Smaks standing on each others heads, but not tall enough for what Suba had in mind. He called on his magic and levitated himself beyond the geysers reach. Or he tried to anyway. As soon as he rose a few feet off the ground, he trembled in the air and dropped to the ground, knocking the wind out of him. He laid there resting for a minute, trying to catch his breath. Suba thought about this new revelation. Suba preferred to think things out rather then rush straight into to things like Brog or Eno would. He thought for a while and realized that this island had some kind of a protection from any levitating magic. He remembered when he was levitating himself across the lava and fell all of a sudden. He still shuddered to think of his close encounter with death that time. So he thought. I won't be able to levitate myself across. He thought back to the time that he had fallen from his levitating magic and remembered what he had done that time. Suba surrounded himself with another ball of earth which was supplied by his surroundings. This one was a bit smaller, except Suba did not need it to travel in comfort or style. He just needed it to get him past the fire geysers. He turned one side transparent like he had done before, and prepared to cross the field of the geysers. He started walking forward, or rather rolling forward. He went past several geysers that erupted right next to him showering him with pieces of molten rock, lava, fire, and dirt. His little ball took all these small tests without a problem. Then, when Suba was starting to get pretty confident and felt like no geyser would ever hit him really hard, a red-hot geyser blasted up right under his feet. The ball that he was in flew into the air and came back down landing right on the spurt of lava. He wasn't to high off the ground but he couldn't get off the fire spurt. The fire slowly began to eat away at the earth at the bottom of his ball. Suba began to get worried. This was the first major test that his ball of earth had ever tried to fight and he knew for a fact that if he did not manage to get of the burst of lava in the air or it did not subside for some time that he would have to get some more earth, water, or his goose was cooked, literally.

Chapter 33
Eno

Eno was shocked by the crystals. When he turned to ask Kanak about them he found him way up ahead. Eno jogged for a while to catch up to him. Kanak was still walking when he turned around and found Eno jogging right behind him pretty much out of breath. "So you managed to keep up with me, eh? Not like those other two I guided through here before. But then there are many ways you are not like anyone or thing I have ever seen before" Kanak said with a twinkle in his eye. Kanak started walking forward and once again, Eno had to jog to keep up with him. Eno marveled at Kanak's ability to go fast with little legs. He could go as fast walking as Eno could jogging. Then a crafty idea came to Eno. He was quite tired by the time he got his idea and it would give him a rest and be funny. Eno used his magic and levitated himself which was one of Suba's and his favorite spells. He flipped over on his back in the air and waited until Kanak had gone some way in front of him, then propelled himself forward. He closed his eyes as he drifted past Kanak, only leaving them open a crack so he could see his reaction. Kanak looked up as Eno passed him, and got a crafty look in his eye. With surprising agility for one so short, Kanak sprinted forward, leaped as high as he could , and landed right on Eno's stomach. Eno dropped a few feet in the air, winded by Kanak's landing. He turned his head and glared at Kanak who was riding on his stomach for a while, but then good-naturedly agreed to carry Kanak if he did not move too much or bother him, and showed the way. Eno closed his eyes again and let Kanak do the directing. Kanak would shout "left" or "right" and Eno would change their course so that they would go that way. Soon it seemed, for neither Eno or Kanak were walking, Kanak said "stop" and Eno stopped, opened his eyes and flipped over flinging Kanak to the floor. Eno floated down laughing at Kanak who had been thrown to the floor but then reached down to try to help him up. Kanak came up laughing with Eno at his little payback for Kanak jumping on his stomach. Kanak turned to look forward and stopped in surprise. Eno followed his gaze and saw that what could have once been the entrance to a tunnel covered by a huge boulder which only let a few cracks of daylight in around the edges of it. Kanak looked at Eno and said "well, I haven't been into this tunnel for a long time and didn't know about this rock here. I'm sorry Eno, I guess you will have to go through the gas somehow. The tribe must have put this rock here. It would be just like them if they somehow found out about this secret passage. Thank the gods one of them didn't come after me. We would have been able to escape being great climbers while they are terrified of heights." Eno was surprised and responded by sending question after question at Kanak.

"Why do they live on a mountain if they are terrified of heights? Are you sure that it was them who put the stone here? Do you think that we should check on your family? We might be able to move the stone don't you think so? Oh what am I saying, I can move it with magic!" So saying, Eno held up his hand and sent a single ray of light striking deep into the rock. Instead of moving it aside however, it shattered the rock apart and sent shards of stone flying everywhere. Eno quickly created a shield and all of the rocks that flew towards him and Kanak bounced right off the air when they weren't that far away from them. Eno held up his shield quite easily actually. The little flying pieces of rock proved to be no challenge whatsoever to him. When all the rocks had stopped flying went out from behind Eno and said "this is it the entrance that you wanted. If you look down the mountain you will see the purple sleeping gas that I was talking about.' Eno stepped out of the tunnel and found himself on a small ledge in the mountain, just big enough for him to stretch out on. He lay down but not before looking over the side of the ledge and seeing the purple gas that Kanak said would put you to sleep while you clung to the mountain and that you would eventually lose your grip and plummet down to your death at the bottom of the mountain and be impaled upon the extremely sharp rocks that littered the bottom of the mountain. Kanak said farewell to him wishing him a good trip and hoped that he would have time to stop on his way down at their house. Eno said that he would try too and with that, Kanak went back down the tunnel. Eno stepped up on the ledge and looked up. The summit was not to far up in front of him. Eno was wondering how far it was up to it and how long it would take him to get there. He started climbing up the mountain wanting to save his magic for later. Once he came to another ledge and took a short rest there. The top seemed only a tiny bit closer and it felt to Eno like he had been climbing for miles and miles. This time though, when he looked up at the summit, he thought he could see a building up there. He brought his vision way up with magic and let himself see all the way to the top of the mountain. What he saw there shocked him. For resting right on the direct center of the summit of the mountain was a shrine and inside that shrine, there was a huge glowing diamond!

Chapter 34
Zimmo

*Z*immo began his story. "Well I am a Smak, that's for sure. I come from a little village where I used to live. My friend Suba had a dream of his father that told him some Klaks would be coming. Suba liked to read a lot of old scrolls and he told no one but me this but I will tell you now. He always wanted to be one of the old Smak heroes. When Klaks invaded this land a long time ago, the three old heroes used three sacred weapons to drive them out. But they were leading a whole Smak army behind them. We have no army. Suba feels like our only hope is to get some army, all the weapons, and Suba's secret belief, more sacred weapons. He thinks that this invasion is going to be even bigger than the last one and we aren't prepared enough for it. Suba sent us out and we after many adventures which included finding some enemies like Ganuf, we split up and each went after a different jewel. That's how I ended up here." Zimmo looked up at the council as he ended his story.

"So please if you have a sapphire that you think might be the one that I am looking for, could you give it to me? If you don't then just tell me and I'll be on my way." Osman shook his head. "No you do not understand. You know of us and you could tell others of your kind and you might even have a wizard or two strong enough to break the lock and get in our forest. I must confer with the other members of the council." Osman turned on his chair to talk to various other animals. After less than thirty seconds he turned back.

"By unanimous vote, this Smak shall walk the deathpath. If he can get past the numerous obstacles that it holds without severely mangling himself or dying, we will assist him to get the sapphire that was stolen from us back. And furthermore we shall try to assemble an army of whatever creatures we can to help you for you said you had no army." Zimmo almost laughed in relief. Here he was thinking that they were going to roast him over an open fire when he finds out that they will let him go free and even help him if he walks their Deathpath. How hard could it be he thought? His views were changed however when he was led to a cave and thrust inside a ledge. It was pitch black and Osman's voice came echoing through the cave. "All you have to do is get past a small obstacle course. It will make a turn when you are halfway through. I wish you good luck for your sake." All of a sudden, glaring lights came on and Zimmo wasn't feeling to confident anymore. Underneath the whole course was a bunch of lava with steep walls that no one living or dead would be able to climb. Anyways, he would be burned alive before he even had a chance to make it to the walls. One slip from the course and he would be fried. Zimmo finally raised his gaze to the course itself. Now he wasn't feeling good at all. In fact he was feeling like these were his last few moments of life. First there were platforms only as wide and long as Zimmo lying down that he had to jump across to get to the first big space where he could stand without fear of falling off the edge. He could see that there were a bunch of trees there. After that he could make out a thin wire going to another big space. Zimmo presumed that the wire was a zip line and that he was supposed to ride it. On that space the curve that signaled that halfway point began. The only problem was that where he landed there were two rows of fire that flickered on and off. There were two more fields like this one with two rows and the middle one with five rows of fire. In between all the fire fields there were crushing walls that slammed together very quickly every few seconds and anything that got caught between them would be squished flatter that a pancake. If he somehow managed to get past all of that he had to do more of the jumping platforms to another big space where there were about fifty arrow blasters on each side that he had no doubt whatsoever would come on and try to zap him as soon as he set a foot on that big space. And if that wasn't enough he had to do some more jumping platforms which would lead to a moving walkway where he had to jump over the electrical fences. Only then was the obstacle course over.

Chapter 35
Fallou

Fallou gasped in surprise and her suit prevented any water from rushing into her mouth. There right in front of her was the topaz that she had been looking for! But she was dragged down by the creature who had one of its tentacles wrapped around her. She thought of her bow and arrows wrapped firmly inside her suit which would do her no good here. She spun around quickly forcing the creature to release her. But it came back and Fallou was quickly set upon by three more creatures. The last one was making a weird sort of noise which would probably bring the others in. If they all came she knew that she would stand no chance whatsoever of escaping with the topaz. The four creatures had her against the wall right above the captain's desk. Fallou thought that she would probably die there being crushed against the wall when she happened to look down at the captain's desk and saw the rusty sword laying there. She was struggling to get free of the creatures but they had left her arms free while two of then pressed their tentacles against her chest, slowly squeezing the life out of her. She reached down, scrabbled around for a few heart stopping seconds, before her hand came to rest against the hilt of the sword. She grabbed it and swung upwards as hard as she could, and since in water it is easier to move and everything weighs less, the sword cut straight through the first creatures' body. Fallou thrust the sword at the next creature holding her before they had time to see what had happened. It went straight through it. But Fallou wasn't very good with a sword. As she turned to face the last three creatures, she realized that the one calling had stopped. All three of the creatures shot their tentacles toward her as she dived forward and came up behind the creatures slashing. Two more were killed before the last one turned to face her. It raised its tentacles and she chucked her sword at it as hard as she could. It flew straight and before the creature could shoot out its tentacles, the sword pierced it right through the middle. It fell down to the floor with the sword still stuck inside of it. Fallou reached down and disdainfully pulled the sword out of its body. Then she swam to the captain's desk and looked at the topaz. She hadn't had the time to look at it before and know she realized that it was really quite beautiful. The only thing she wondered about was how a topaz of that size would fit into the hilt of a sword. She picked it up and she was answered. The topaz shrank to the size of a tiny marble which she could roll around in her hand, but it did not lose any of is brilliancy. She knew that she had to leave now before the other creatures came in looking for her. She reached in and opened a hatch in her suit and stored it there. She was about leave when she saw five blue tipped lances lying on the floor. She thought that they must have been from the five creatures that she had killed. She strapped them onto her back for throwing and put one in her left hand for stabbing with. Her right hand held the sword that she had picked up from the captain's desk. She quickly went back out the door. She hoped that the creatures would be so much dazed that they would allow her to get back to the surface of the water or at least close to it. She went back through another room and saw the cavern where she could get out from. If she had been on land, she would probably have jumped about, shouting with jubilation, but she was underwater here and the need for silence was so great that she could barely afford to step on a splinter in the wreck for it might let out a squeak and give her away to the creatures. She peeked around a jutting edge of wood and saw with horror the blue creatures streaming into the hole. One raised a tentacle and pointed right where she was and beckoned for the others to go on. Hundreds after hundreds were streaming through the hole and now they were all headed for Fallou. She raised the lance she was holding and thrust it forward with all her might. It struck the lead creature and she watched as blue electricity crackled down its length. But now they were throwing lances at her!

Chapter 36
Brog

Brog stared in horror as the giant's icy breath covered him. He began to feel his limbs turning to ice, the blood freezing in his veins. He tried to move or shout but found that he could do neither. All of a sudden he had a sudden irresistible urge to sleep. He could not fight it no matter how hard he tried. Then everything went black as he started to sleep. The next thing he felt was like his arm was on fire. He yanked as hard as he could and hit something cold and icy. In a flash it all came back to him. The fight with the ice giants. The one blowing on him. The horrible feeling of turning to ice. He slowly and gently wiggled to see if he was still frozen and found that he could move his limbs again. None were frozen anymore. He turned to the giant he knew was standing next to him and reached down to grab his axe. He stopped in shock. It wasn't there. Neither was his shield. He turned to run but found a boiling pot of extremely hot water behind him. Then he realized that he was in a hut of some kind. He turned to another wall and saw the ice giant. Behind it was his axe, shield, and the door that he needed to use to escape. Before he could launch himself around it, it spoke in harsh, grating tones. "You may leave if you wish. But I would not attempt it if I were you. For instance, did you know that there are many ice giants guarding this door day and night? Did you know that I am your friend in this place and not truly an ice giant? Did you know that you would have been dead and eaten in some ice giant's belly if I had not saved you?" and saying that, the ice giant reached up one massive icy hand to the back of its neck and pulled a zipper that let all the ice fall off of it. There standing in front of him was a Smak. Brog was totally speechless. He stood slack-jawed staring at the Smak. The Smak smiled.

"Yes indeed I am your friend. We are in an ice castle of the giants. You don't stand even the tiniest chance of escaping yourself. I will help you escape. But first tell me, how did you get here?" Brog told his story ending at the part where he felt the giants breath coming down across him. He told the Smak that he was looking for a ruby. The Smak said "a ruby you say? I know of only one such gem and it is set in the king's crown. You couldn't steal it if you had a whole army behind you. The only way that you are going to get the crown is by challenging the king to combat. Whoever wins gets the crown. But before you go charging outside you must know that the fight will most probably be to the death. And that we do not chose our king by votes. We chose our king by determining who is the strongest, fastest, smartest, and most cunning of all. One last thing that you must know is that an ice giant's only weakness is"—"I know behind the knees" interrupted Brog roughly. "Just give me back my shield and axe and I will declare a challenge to the death. The only thing is that I need to be alone for some time to prepare. And if you have any armor that would fit me I would be much obliged." As Brog finished talking the other Smak hurried outside to find a suit of armor. Brog could hear him talking to the guards. He crossed over the floor to his axe and shield and quickly picked them up. He crossed back over to the pot of boiling water. He took out his axe, hefted it, and lifted the pot off the fire. He dropped his shield onto the fire followed by his axe. He ate the meal that the other Smak had prepared for him and since there was not much else to do, he went to sleep. When he woke up, the other Smak was still not back. Brog began to be worried thinking that he would never come back and that he had been duped. He looked out of the door by opening it just a crack and saw a figure talking to the ice giant guards. It was the other Smak! Brog crossed over the room and picked up a stick that lay next to the fire. He quickly pulled his shield and axe out of the fire and turned around just as the other Smak came in the door holding some armor. Brog thanked the Smak and tried on the armor. It fit him perfectly. He tried not to look too pleased. The other Smak said that if he was going to offer a challenge that he had better do it now. Brog understood and stood up. The Smak told him exactly how to go about it. He would have to yell as loud as he could that he wanted to challenge the king.

He would have to yell it a few times before the ice giants saw him and would freeze him again. Then everything would be lost. He would keep on yelling till someone took him to see the king. His axe's blade had almost melted from being in the fire for so long. He could manage to carry his shield even though it was also hot. He went out side and almost immediately an ice giant grabbed him and started marching him somewhere. Brog managed to get one arm free enough to drag his axe in the snow for only a little while because he only wanted it to cool down a bit, he wanted his weapons to be burning hot for the encounter with the king. All of a sudden the surroundings changed. He was in the castle but in a large stadium. The scene changed again to a much smaller stadium which Brog would much prefer to fight on. Their was a huge crowd in the stands. They were all their to see the puny little Smak get crushed by their king. Brog thought that the outcome of the match would be much different then they were thinking!

Chapter 37
Suba

Suba looked around in a panic as crazy and crazier thoughts popped into his head. He looked down and put his hand on the earth of his ball. It was weakening very fast. Soon all of it would be gone. He couldn't find anywhere to get more earth. He looked down again just in time to see the bottom of his ball give way and lava come rushing in. He jumped up just before the lava could scorch him, blasted through the roof of the ball of earth, and catapulted out to the ground breaking his landing with a roll. All around him geysers were springing up and he was dodging to the left and right trying not to get hit. Then a great geyser sprung up right in front of him. This geyser was remarkable because of its sheer size and the heat it gave off. It seemed to shoot up into infinity never stopping. It was as wide as Suba was tall. Suba rolled to the left, sprung up, and walked past the geyser. The sight that next greeted Suba made him happy. For the field of geysers had ended and Suba had made it out in one piece. Sure he had some minor burns from the lava in his ball of dirt, but it was nothing much. Suba got up from where he sat on the ground, dusted himself off, and looked up. What he saw shocked him. Standing right in front of him, a good ten or twelve feet tall, was the biggest spider that Suba had ever seen or heard about! He leaped backwards twisting in midair and landed catlike on all fours away from the spider. Suba raised his hand and it glowed with a ball of pure magic energy. The spider held up one claw and spoke in a deep resonating voice that shocked Suba so much he almost fell over flat. *"Come little one put your magic away. It will not hurt me. Now follow me. I have something that may interest you."* And since he had nothing better to do, Suba lowered his hand slightly and followed the spider.

Chapter 38
Eno

*E*no sat and rested a while on that ledge to get his strength back. While he was doing that he pondered what he had seen. He had seen a shrine on the direct center of the mountaintop. The only problem with his first plan of just walking up the mountain and seizing it was that he had also seen several hundred huts surrounding the shrine on the side of the mountain. He had almost no chance of walking straight through and not coming to any harm let alone surviving. The best plan that he could come up with was that he would wait until night and then try to sneak past while everyone who lived in the village was sleeping. He leaped up with renewed vigor at the thought of creeping past whoever slept in those huts and stealing their diamond from right under their nose. Finally Eno got tired of climbing again and got so frustrated that he could not make it to much farther up the mountain that he lifted himself with magic and threw himself. He literally flew. Since he had his shield wrapped firmly on his back when he hit an up draft after he finally stopped falling, it acted like a parachute and carried him upwards since he had made it extremely light with magic. Eno noticed this and created an even stronger updraft using magic. His shield carried him upwards very fast. Eno had barely sufficient time to rest when he realized that he was almost to the start of the villages. He stopped the updraft and let himself drift to the ground slowly. As soon as he hit the ground he rolled behind a cluster of rocks. Up ahead he could see the lights of the village dimming as night fell. Eno jumped up from behind his rock after giving it a few more hours to make sure that everyone was asleep. When he was sure of this he strolled jauntily into the village. He did not see the guards though until it was almost to late. He dived backwards and rolled around his pile of rocks again. He had gotten a good look at the guards and had seen that each one carried a spear a sword a shield and a mace. Good thought Eno. They might put up a fight with all those weapons but they have just what I need. Also each guard had a lantern laying on the ground next to him. However, the guard in front of Eno had just dropped his sword to pick up the lantern. Good news thought Eno. He levitated himself with magic until he was right above the guards head then dropped his mace point right into the guard's head from above. The guard went down without a sound or cry. Eno dropped swiftly, yanked the spear out of the dead guards' hands and propped him up on it. That was the only time he had a chance to get a good look at the creature. Eno had to cover his mouth with his hand to stop from gasping out for the creature was a Smak. Eno grimly levitated himself over to the next guard and repeated the maneuver. He did this to every guard that there was. He did not find a single one of them that was not a Smak. Now that he had finished off all the guards it was a simple matter for Eno to go ahead and walk into the village. He started running forward, tripped over a snag in the ground. He let out a yell and then starting cursing himself for his foolishness. Had he forgotten that he needed to be quiet? That he was creeping into a village in the dead of the night? That he had just killed all twenty-four of the village guards? He jumped to his feet called on his magic and began flying as fast as he could go towards the shrine at the top of the mountain. But people were already piling out of their homes to see what was going on and what the yell was about. Eno looked around wildly hoping to see one creature, any creature that was not a Smak. But his search came to a dead end. By now Smaks had rubbed the sleep from their eyes and were pointing and shouting in amazement, fear, and anger as Eno sped by them. He dodged their outstretched hands which kept on reaching for him turning and twisting desperately in midair, hoping, hoping that it was all a bad nightmare and that he would wake up soon. But he knew that he would find no waking to this nightmare as he dodged. For this was no nightmare to Eno. It was actually the real thing. All of a sudden he turned a corner and saw the diamond right in front of him. That was his last vision before everything went black.

Chapter 39
Zimmo

Zimmo stared at the course for a while and then surprised everyone including himself by making a leap onto the first platform. He just managed to make it. Just as he started nerving himself for the next jump, the platform started to shake and began to fall. Zimmo was shaken by this and took his leap a bit too early. It was only some quick thinking that saved him. As he noticed himself begin to fall short of the ledge, he reached back in midair and brought his shield out. As he was falling, he reached up as high as he could and hooked the edge of his shield onto the edge of the platform. It kept him from falling temporarily. But then the platform that he had his shield hooked onto began to shake. Zimmo thought quickly again. Bringing out some rope that he had been given, he made a firm knot around the holding part of his spear. He did all of this while keeping one hand on his shield to hold him up. He then managed to yank himself up on top of the ledge just as it began to fall. Then he took careful aim with his spear as the platform he was on fell towards the lava that was under him. Then he drew back his arm and threw his spear as hard as he could. It arced perfectly and landed right on top of the next platform. Lucky for him there was not to much of rope so he did not have to climb to far up it to reach the next platform. He hauled himself over the edge and yanked his spear out of the wood just as it began to shake. He groaned and muttered "not again" before gathering up his spear and hurling it again. This time however after he repeated the maneuver that he had used to get on the platform, it was a pretty big ledge and on it there was a forest. It did not look too forbidding and there did not seem to be any traps in the trees or on the ground when he checked. So he walked in confidently enough. He walked through the forest with nothing bad happening to him. He walked all the way to the end of the ledge feeling only a little bit more tired than usual. Then he saw a zip line. But when he saw his arm he was very scared. For hanging onto it were leeches! They were all over his body! He jumped down and rolled on the ground. The leeches were eventually shaken off and the others he had to spear off. Then he went back to the zip line and rode it. It put him on another ledge. This one was almost comforting in a way because he could see the danger to begin with and knew that there was no chance of a hidden danger in the field. The bad news was that the danger was pretty big. Right where he would land was a field of fire that would flick on and off randomly. He got past this pretty easily but almost got crushed by some slamming walls.

He only escaped when he managed to climb over them. Then he ran straight into another field of fire. He was not expecting this and he was burned a little bit before the fire went off again. Then he passed some more slamming walls by climbing over them and one more fire field. Then there was a clear space to help him prepare his jump for some more platforms. Beyond that he could see the course change directions. He had reached the halfway point.

Chapter 40
Fallou

Fallou dodged back behind the wood except it did not look so graceful underwater. She listened as the thump of several lances hitting the wall which she was hiding behind continued without a break. Fallou knew that they were going to keep her pinned down there until at least some of the creatures could travel through the great chamber. Fallou hoped that it would take them a while and it might since the chamber was huge. But then the creatures were very good swimmers. Meanwhile she would try to think of a plan. She couldn't go out of her cover because of the constant hail of lances. She looked around and to her surprise, she found a small passageway that she had definitely not seen before. Since she had almost no choice whatsoever she went in with her little propellers moving her forward. She found that the passageway curved for a while. Then she turned her propellers on to the highest speed that they could go because she was getting afraid that the creatures would come after her. Instantly she sped up. It was like she was riding on a horse and was going too fast. Soon she could see the end of the passageway and because of the speed that she was going at, it did not much surprise her to see the end of the tunnel so soon. She stopped right before she went out of the tunnel and cautiously poked her head out just in case any more of the creatures were near. None were. Fallou popped out and realized where she was. She was proud. After all, she had dived to the depths of the ocean, found alien creatures that blew up her ship, invade their layer while they were out, killed six of them, stolen a precious jewel, and escaped their ambush alive. She had reasons to be proud. But she could not resist going back to the entrance hole of the ship and one last glimpse of the creatures and their attempts to find her. The creatures had made it to the wall and were searching for her. No doubt they would search the captains' room and probably all of the other rooms once they could not find her. She laughed inside her helmet. Their search would be futile. She was watching them from behind. The next thing she noticed was the wall. It was stuck full of blue electric lances that the creatures had been throwing. She also noticed that they were almost out of their lances. Without waiting to find out what their reaction would be when they found that their victim or prey or whatever it was that she was going to be was not there, she was propelled by her propellers upwards. When she had gone for a while she happened to look back down. She saw five blue creatures with one leading them, following her. They hadn't been able to catch her yet, but Fallou felt that she had better get rid of them. But as she watched the leader was taken away by a shark. But that still left five of them following her. She turned and dived back down and thrust through two of them with the sword and the shot up before they could grab her. But they were now close. She turned and threw the sword. Now there was only one following her. It would have caught her except she broke the surface of the water and was swept to a friendly shore by a current.

Chapter 41
Brog

Brog's resolve was put to the test when a gigantic ice giant stepped up onto the stage. He wore no armor but carried a shield in one hand and a wicked looking icicle-spear in the other hand. Brog was scared nearly out of his wits. The giant seemed to think of Brog as an animal or worse. He raised his hand up high and the crowd went wild. They were all cheering for him thought Brog. Well I'll show all of them, they're going to be leaving with very different opinions. He went up to the king and roared for all of those watching to hear "when is the death match for you going to start you lily-livered scum? I'll finish it quick if you are apologizing and groveling on your knees to me. Otherwise I promise I'll make the pain last as long as I can." Brog reached back to grab his axe handle and felt the burning heat of his weapons that he had cooked up to counter the freezing cold of the ice giant king. The king roared back "as soon as you wish it. In fact I propose now and it will be you who is groveling to me for your life." He took a swipe at Brog but Brog was expecting it and leaped backwards dodging it easily. "Come on, is that the best you can do" he cried. The ice giant leaped forward with a huge roar and the battle began in earnest with the crowd of giants oohing and aahing. But the battle was soon to be over. For as the giant leaped at him Brog drew his axe, rolled on the ground, and slashed up with his burning axe. He felt it sink into the giants' stomach, and instead of sending off chips of ice, it left a long deep gash and the giant doubled over in pain. Brog leaped up behind the giant king and gave a quick slash to both of his knees. The ice giant king who had never been beaten before had just been beaten by a small Smak named Brog. The crowd stared in stunned silence. Then a cheer slowly began. The crowd was chanting his name. He did not have time to figure out how they had found out his name. Brog, Brog BRog, BRog, BROg, BROg, BROG, BROG, BROG, BROG. Brog wasn't sure what to do and tentively raised his hand.. This got a roar from the crowd. Brog smiled and laughed. He turned to the fallen king and gently took the crown off his head. Then he called for some ice giant healers and was surprised to see them coming and kneeling to him. He told them to help their old king. They carried him off to a room. Then Brog turned the crown around and found the ruby in it. He took it out and raised his hands for silence. The giants immediately fell silent. "I have an announcement to make" said Brog. "I did not truly want the position of the ice giant king. No, all I wanted was a small ruby and my freedom. Believe me, you will be under better rule with your regular king rather than me. So I have taken the ruby that was set in the crown and I leave it here for your king. With that I bid you, farewell." And Brog turned, marched up to the gate, opened it, and went outside to his freedom turning around one last time and he thought he saw the fake ice giant wave to him.

Chapter 42
Suba

The spider took Suba into a small hole. It went underground and opened up into a vast cavern. What Suba saw their amazed him and continued to amaze him as he later looked back upon his life. He saw a cavern piled high with treasure. In fact their was enough treasure to last a lifetime. But when Suba looked carefully, he found something that shocked him so much that he gasped with surprise. Lying right next to him was the emerald that he had been searching for for so long. He started forward and was about to grab it when he realized that the spider was calling him. He turned slowly, thinking that it would not be wise to disobey a twelve foot tall, predatory spider, especially when you were in its lair and probably about to become a tasty snack. The spider said "I see that you have found my emerald. Or should I say the one that you are seeking? But I will not give it up without a fight. Sure I am on your side but I cannot give you the emerald without you having to at least prove to me that you are worthy of having it, an honorable person, a person who would not lose it on the way back. The only thing I ask you to do is fight me, but if you win, please on my request, do not kill me. Just forcing me to admit defeat will be sufficient. And if I do not you may proceed with killing me." Suba took out his sword even though he knew it would not be much of a weapon, and before the spider could say anything else, or he changed his mind, Suba went into action. He leaped forward to the spider bringing his sword flying through the air in a killer arc. But the spider lowered its head and Suba's sword met horns that Suba had not seen before with a metallic *zing!* Suba landed on his feet right under the spider. He brought his sword in a sweeping arc over his head and felt it cut into the spider's soft belly. A deep black liquid dripped out of the cut that Suba had made. The spider roared in frustration, anger, and pain. It rolled over leaving Suba expose with nowhere to hide. Suba tried the same maneuver that he had used before except this time the spider knew it was coming. It raised one gigantic black leg and swiped Suba away. Suba flew backwards and lay on his back, winded. The spider came over and opened his mouth to reveal huge teeth. But Suba rolled to the side just as the spider lunged. All it got for its efforts was a mouthful of ground. Suba jumped to his feet and slashed down with his sword. It met one leg and lopped it off. The spider lifted its head and roared with agony. This was the moment Suba needed. He threw himself in front of the spider and slashed wildly, blindly, and madly at the spider in front of him with fury. His strokes came lightning-fast and were impossible to block. The spider tried backing away but Suba followed still slashing till the spider was in a corner. The sword was cutting deep furrows into the spider. Finally, it had to admit defeat. It went to someplace to nurse its heavy wounds. Suba went over and made his tired arms pick up the emerald. At last Suba had gotten the emerald.

Chapter 43
Eno

The first thing that Eno saw when he woke up was that he was still outside and that it was still night. He tried to bring his hands up but realized that they were tied. That was when he heard the harsh laughter. He found that he could still move his head a bit, and by turning it a fraction he saw that the laughter was coming from the crowd of villagers. They poked him with long sticks that were pointed at the top. Their little jabs hurt a ton. He finally cried out after trying hard not to let these cruel village Smaks see that he was in pain. There was a cry from the audience and the jabs came harder than ever. At last Eno had had enough. He burned through the ropes with magic and then shot a tremor through the ground that knocked everyone off their feet. While everyone was still trying to get to their feet and figure out what had happened, Eno jumped up and ran forward blasting a way through the crowd by hitting anything in front of him with a tremendous blast of wind that would knock you flying backwards. As a consequence, several people were blown far away. Eno took a turn and there it was just as he remembered. There was the shrine with the diamond inside of it. He ran up the steps, grabbed the diamond and tucked it under his arm like a football runner. He only barely managed to stop when he saw that he was on the edge of a great canyon that fell down into nothingness. He slowly backed away. He turned around and prepared to sprint back down the steps back into the village, when he saw that the villagers had gathered their wits and trapped him against the edge of the canyon. They held the long poles that they had been using to poke him with. They were advancing on him. All of a sudden, he smiled and said "I hope you guys have fun, but I've been here to long. It's time for me to go." With that said, he turned and jumped of the edge of the cliff into the canyon. The crowd gasped and lunged forward to stop him. But he was already gone. Then he caused an updraft that made him float back up level to the villagers. They were amazed only for a minute. One ingenious inventive person threw his long pole at Eno. Eno dodged it and laughed but his laughter was cut off as someone had thrown another pole and this one had hit his arm. He wrenched it out and threw it back. But then everyone else who was holding a pole had gotten the idea and began chucking their poles at him. He dodged down below the cliff and watched as their poles passed harmlessly overhead. He then went into a free fall down the mountain. He turned over so he could see what was coming up. What he saw was the side of the mountain coming rapidly closer. He got ready and right when he was about to hit the mountain, sent a huge updraft of wind. It gently set him down on the mountainside. Since it was beginning to lighten up, Eno could see that he was next to Kanak's cave. He thought that he had time to drop by and pay the friendly little creatures a visit.

Chapter 44
Zimmo

*Z*immo easily cleared the jumping platforms and watched them as they fell away. This time he had not even had to use his makeshift grappling hook. But then his feet touched down on the next big platform and as if on cue, the blasters that were surmounted on the walls came on. Zimmo dropped to the floor which was the only safe place. The blasters passed harmlessly over his head, their deadly poisoned arrows just missing him.. He also realized that if he wanted to stay alive in this deadly crossfire of arrows, he would have to crawl all the way to the other side of the platform. It was tedious work but he finally managed to make it to the other side. And when he did, the arrows stopped. Zimmo stood warily ready to through himself right back down if there was even the slightest sign of the arrows coming back on again. He threw himself forward onto some more jumping platforms, but was off balance because at every moment of his jump he was expecting the arrows to come back on again and hit him. But they didn't and he saved himself by using his makeshift grappling hook again. He threw it up and watched as it latched onto the next jumping platform. He used it once more to get onto the next and final big platform. The only problem was that as soon as he landed he found himself on a moving walkway. He almost lost his balance but recovered it just in time to see an electrical fence crackling across the walkway. He leaped about a foot in the air in surprise and that was what saved him from being zapped. He jumped right over the fence and landed on the walkway on the other side of it. But he quickly realized that he wasn't saved yet. For he saw three more electric fences ahead of him. The first two he navigated with ease. But the last one was a different matter. For when he was only a few yards away from the fence, he saw the finish line. The sight of it threw him of balance again. By the time he regained his balance, he was only a few feet away from the fence. He knew that he would not be able to get a good jump from his position. It was too close to the fence. So he tried to run back on the moving walkway except in turned out that if he tried to run backwards the moving walkway got faster and all that he would do was run in place. While he was doing this, making no headway whatsoever against the moving walkway, he took out his rope and threw it. It flew far but instead of latching on to anything it fell into an electric fence and was fried. Zimmo decided to chance jumping since he would get fried if he waited too long. He jumped higher than he ever had before and just managed to flip over it. He landed on the moving pathway except this time he did not have to worry about anything. There were no more electric fences, no more leeches, no more fires and slamming walls. All that was left was the finish line. He lay down on the walkway because he was so tired. The walkway carried him over the finish line just as he got back to his feet. He cheered and raised his hands in the air as he was carried out of the oppressive gloom of the obstacle course cave into bright sunlight where there were all the animals waiting and watching this weird screen that showed the obstacle course and what Zimmo was doing when they saw him come out of the cave they gave a great cheer. Zimmo was surprised what they were cheering about for he was almost certain that all the animals there had wanted him to die in the obstacle course. But then he saw Osman who said "you made it! I know you think we wanted you to lose but our customs say that is what you must feel. Everything we did including the trial was a fake." Osman then took out a sapphire and presented it to Zimmo stared at it, smiled, looked around at the animals and said "thanks guys." He rubbed the sapphire against the necklace that Sobask had given him and started teleporting back.

Chapter 45
Fallou

Fallou rested for a while on the shore where she had landed after being chased by the blue alien creatures. After she had rested enough, she got up. She shrugged off the suit that she was wearing and opened the pouch in which she had left the topaz. It gleamed in the light as it easily slid out of the wet pouch. Fallou watched as light reflected and refracted off the tiny water droplets on it and the gem itself. She stuck it into her pocket and took out the necklace that Sobask had given each of them. He said that when they had found their jewel, all they had to do was rub the jewel against the half moon stone that was set in the necklace. She took out the topaz again and carefully rubbed it against the moon. Nothing happened. She put her topaz away and started to look up just as she felt a tug and was flying through space. She was flipped upside down, turned around, spun out of control, and hurtled through space and time. She was hoping for the journey to end and also hoping for her topaz not to fall out. She could not reach down and make sure that her topaz was safe because she was being flipped around so much that she did not know which way was up or down, or where the rest of her body was. Once she felt for her arm and tried to reach down with it. It moved, she could tell that much but she could not tell or see where. All her senses were clogged. She could see colors flashing past as if she was in a tunnel of colors. She could hear tumultuous music that crashed over it. She could feel nothing whatsoever so that was not much help to her. She could actually taste things, though she figured that her brain was probably just doing that to her. She could smell many different things but mainly the smell off earth after a rainstorm. All of a sudden she had a falling sensation and the next thing that she knew was that she had landed on something hard. She opened her eyes to see, nothing. Or rather, a brown nothing. Fallou pushed herself up and realized what had happened. She had not gone temporarily blind. She had been laying face-down on the ground and when she had opened her eyes she saw ground. She moved her head up which was a great effort because her body was still disorientated from the wild ride to get back to Sobask. For she saw Sobask in front of her. She raised her hand weakly to acknowledge that she had seen him. Sobask asked with a smirk on his face if she had had a nice ride. She grinned, reached back, grabbed an arrow, and threw it at Sobask. It hit him on the nose and he grunted in surprise. She laughed and slowly got to her feet. She immediately had to sit down again. Her head was still spinning from the wild ride. She settled down to wait for her head and body to stop spinning around and get reoriented. She then settled herself for the longer wait of waiting for the others to find their gems and make it back.

Chapter 46
Brog

Brog marched through the gate still holding the ruby. He heard the gates slam behind him but still did not turn around. Then at last after he had walked for a while he stopped and turned around. Then he saw the Smak that had helped him to escape running towards him. He turned around and sat down in the snow waiting for the other Smak to catch up to him. Soon the Smak came to Brog puffing from his hard run to catch up to him. Brog smiled when the Smak turned up and asked if the Smak wanted to go with him. The Smak said "no I do not want to go with you. I came to say goodbye and wish you good luck. Also I came to tell you that I need to stay here and help the ice giants get back to normal. I mean it's not everyday we get a visitor who walks in the door, overthrows the king, and then walks out leaving the king to claim his title again. I will stay behind and help the ice giants. But I will call for you if I need your help. Farewell." Brog smiled at the Smak as it started to run off. Only then did Brog realize that he had never found out what the Smak's name was. Then he started wondering how he was going to get back. He thought that maybe if he went right back to the point that Sobask had teleported him from maybe he would be teleported right back. Or if that didn't work maybe he would be able to see the fire-mountain rising in the distance from the top of the mountain. So Brog started trekking through the snow back to the mountain which he could clearly see. It seemed to be very close. In fact it seemed to be so close that it would take him almost no time whatsoever to reach it. However if something is really big it may seem like it is right next to you, but it could be really far away. In fact, it might even take you days to reach it. That is the way it was with the mountain and Brog. He had thought that it would hardly take him any time whatsoever to reach the mountain but night came and he had still not reached it. And with every step he took, the big half moon necklace that Sobask had given him bumped uncomfortably. Sobask had told them all that they could do something with it except that Brog hadn't really been listening when Sobask had said that. Anyways it couldn't have been that important. All he had said that after you got the gem that you were looking for you could do something with it to take you back. Brog had figured that it was a kind of compass and would lead you in the direction that you were going. So far it had been doing nothing of the sort though. Brog had begun to get doubtful that he would reach the mountain by nightfall and his suspicions were confirmed. So Brog being tired from a long day of endless plodding, cleared a space on the ground of snow and was ready to flop down and get a good night's rest. But as soon as he flipped over onto his back, the ruby that he had put in a pouch brushed against the half moon necklace. Immediately, Brog took the wild ride that Fallou had taken and landed next to her. Fallou laughed and helped him sit up.

Chapter 47
Suba

Suba stared at the emerald happily. He had finally found it. He had thought that it was going to take him years to find it. And then when the spider said that it had it except that Suba would have to fight him for it. Suba had thought that he was dead several times over while fighting the spider yet it turned out that he had lived through it and defeated the spider. That is why Suba felt like jumping about and yelling happily that he had gotten the emerald. He couldn't wait to get back to find the others and tell them about his amazing adventures. He wondered how he was going to get back for a little bit. Then he wondered if he should take any of the treasures in the cave with him. If he ever got back to a normal life after all of this was over he might need some wealth to help him get by in the world. Perhaps even some souvenirs from his old journeying days. He grabbed as much gold as he could carry and a lot of weird shaped or looking trinkets. He then went outside the cave always keeping an eye out for the spider in case it came back for him. It might not have taken kindly to the fact that Suba, a small, puny little Smak had beaten him. Suba trudged back across the barren dry landscape to the field of fire geysers. Suba really didn't feel or have the strength to deal with them right then. So he sat down and rested while trying to think of an alternative solution to get around the field. Unfortunately, no brilliant spark of inspiration appeared like it had been appearing in the past few days. But when he turned around he saw something that made him leap up right away and start charging recklessly into the field of geysers. For what he had seen behind him was the spider at the head of a small army of goblinlike creatures. They were marching straight towards him. Suba assumed that the spider had changed its mind about giving him the emerald and seemed to want it back. Except this time the spider was not alone. It would fight him with a whole army of creatures behind it. Suba knew that if he even somehow managed to defeat the spider again which was very unlikely, the spider would just order the creatures to attack him. Sure he might kill some of them, but if nothing else, the weight of their bodies would eventually crush him. Still they would probably subdue him. That's when it hit him. He could fight the spider if he had to, and he had faith that he would be able to beat him again. But then he could get rid of the creatures with magic. He could bring up a tidal wave of fire if he needed to. It would incinerate every one of them with one little strike. The only reason he couldn't use magic against the spider was that it probably also knew magic and would crush him like a leaf it he tried. So he couldn't use his magic for fear of prompting the spider to use his. And Suba really didn't want to be crushed like a leaf. So he realized that he would have to defeat the spider with his sword and mind only. Anyways he might not even have to fight them if he could get away. All the time that he was thinking this he was dodging like mad. Only one fire geyser had even come close to burning him. Then he got a crafty idea. He used magic to let himself be able to move faster and he breezed by all of the geysers in a blur. He stopped for a moment and turned around. He saw a huge blur heading right for him. It took a while but Suba finally realized that the blur was the spider and his followers speeded up. And they were coming right for him. By now they were already halfway across the field and almost to the end where Suba stood resting. Suba immediately started running hyper fast again. He practically flew down to the banks of the fire ocean where he realized his mistake. He couldn't levitate himself across! He'd have to do it the old way he thought. He looked back and saw that the spider and his minions had just gotten out of the field of fire geysers. He looked desperately around and saw a machine that said Magic Reflector Unit. Suba smashed it with one light blast and tried to levitate himself. It worked! He flew across the fire ocean. Suba grabbed the emerald and teleported himself back to Sobask.

Chapter 48
Eno

*E*no thought that he might as well stop at Kanak's house before teleporting back to Sobask. So he hiked the short way over the mountain to his house. But when he got to the ledge where Kanak's house was, he had the same problem that he had had last time he was climbing up. He got stuck in a place where there were no handholds or footholds except for the ones that he was already holding on to. He thought that he should call for Kanak but then decided that he wanted to surprise his little friend by dropping in. and when Eno thought of dropping in, he meant *dropping* in. he used magic and let himself float till he got right above the entrance. Then he let the magic go and shouted surprise as he landed in the doorway. But his cries fell on deaf ears. Kanak and his family could not hear him. An avalanche or a rockslide had blocked the entrance to their cave completely. There was no way whatsoever that anyone could get in. Then while he was sobbing on the ground, Eno realized that there was a way to get in. He could get in. He could use magic and blast a way in but first he would have to warn Kanak and his family to get away from the door if they were trapped inside. He magnified his voice. Then he shouted through the rocks and into the cave for anyone who was inside to stand back. Eno could hear his cries echoing around inside the cavern. He hoped that they had heard because he did not hear any movement or shuffling of feet that signified that people were moving away from the door. Eno stood a little way back from the door since rock chips could come flying at him and put up a protective barrier in case a rock chip managed to fly that far. If any did they would just bounce right off of his barrier. Eno started blasting the rock with blasts of darkness and light. The rock chips started flying everywhere. Some of them managed to get past the boundaries that he had thought impossible. It seemed that these rock chips were magical blades at from the distance and at the speed that they came at him. He was starting to make a dent in the rock and several rock chips had already hit his barrier. One even came through a little bit but it didn't get far since going through the barrier seemed to have slowed its speed down to normal. Anyway, when Eno stopped for a break he looked at the chip that had gotten through. It looked exactly like a dagger. In fact it was a dagger. It was so sharp and was spinning so fast that it had managed to break through his barrier of protective magic. Eno knew that he would have to stop to rest like this several times along the way. But he knew that he had to blast through the rock to save his friends. He could wait a little bit before teleporting to Sobask. But he couldn't wait at all if he was going to save Kanak and his family. Eno was just ready to start blasting away at the rock again, when he saw a sign. Curious, he went over to look. It wasn't often that you saw a sign in the mountains. It said that Kanak had left because it was getting dangerous. Eno felt like such a fool. He took out the diamond, held it, and teleported to Sobask.

Chapter 49

Eno appeared with all of the others already there. Suba laughed and asked "so you decided to show up for the party. Trust you to smell food and come running." Eno replied "not more so than you. When did you get here, huh?" Suba stuttered "um, um, a little bit before you got here." The others were rolling on the ground, cracking up. Suba smiled and said "alright, alright we're even. But did you get the diamond?" A hush fell over Zimmo, Brog, and Fallou and they stopped rolling around. Eno smiled and said "of course. The only thing I regret is that you managed to beat me!" Everyone started laughing again. Then Sobask came over. He gave a silent nod and everyone stood up and brought out the gems that they were holding. They were stunning by themselves. But then, as if by an unspoken agreement, they all stuck their gem in the slot that was made for them at the beginning of time. There was a blinding flash of light and everyone except Suba flinched away.

When they opened their eyes they saw an incredible sight. The sword was flaming! They had completed their quest for the flaming sword! Everyone danced about cheering. Even Sobask joined in. but in the middle of the festivities, Suba sat down and looked at his friends who were so happy. Their faces were lit up by the glow of the sword. But Suba wondered when would it end, and how many of his beloved friends would survive. But as soon as he thought that he realized that he did not remember Zimmo arriving or him saying much since he had appeared!

To be Continued....